LOVER'S WRATH

AN ANGEL AND HER DEMONS: BOOK THREE

LACEY CARTER ANDERSEN

DEDICATION

To my crew- you know who you are, and you know you're awesome.

~ Lacey Carter Andersen

CONNECT WITH LACEY

Want to be part of the writing process? Maybe even get a taste of my sense of humor? Teasers for my new releases? And more?

Facebook Group: https://www.facebook.com/groups/laceysrealm
Facebook Page: https://www.facebook.com/authorlaceycarterandersen
Pinterest: https://www.pinterest.com/laceycarterandersen/
Twitter: https://twitter.com/LaceyCAndersen
Website: https://laceycarterandersen.net

1

Tristan would never consider himself a liar, but he'd lied to Surcy and Daniel. He'd told them that they could focus on saving the Immortals *and* have a chance to rescue Mark in time. *Which is impossible.*

The instant Caine saw Mark's soul, he would destroy it. There was no question. The druid, who was like a brother to Tristan, would be gone forever. The knowledge clawed within him, screaming in protest.

Gargoyles protected the people they loved. They died before they allowed their loved ones to hurt in any way. The fact that Mark was dead meant he failed.

He *failed.*

A scream built in his throat, a roar of protest and denial. Mark was kind and good. A man who was still ruled by the lost boy who'd been thrown out by his people at such a fragile age. He had seen the worst in the world and still had a heart of gold. Mark was something precious, and Tristan had been sleeping when he died.

Sleeping. It seemed impossible. How could he have slept?

If Tristan didn't do something, he was going to snap. He was going to lose his mind. All his logic was slipping away, replaced by a heart-wrenching emotion he couldn't escape.

As Daniel and Surcy dressed and equipped themselves with weapons to rescue the first Immortal, Tristan slipped out of their home, his heart racing. He needed to find a place to let loose, to let the scream building inside of him explode. He needed to level everything around him to the ground.

Because Mark is dead.

Because I failed him.

Soaring over the gardens and above the quiet city, Tristan felt something cold on his cheek. Reaching up and touching the hard stone of his gargoyle skin, he saw liquid on his fingertip.

Stopping on the edge of a building, he stared at it in confusion.

He didn't understand. He was a gargoyle. Gargoyles couldn't cry. *Can we?*

He was made of stone, and stone didn't weep. And yet, the tear rested on his fingertip as if to remind him of the one flaw of his kind. Despite being made of stone, they had very real hearts.

If only there was something I could do. Anything...

He stiffened, his mind snapping to something he'd nearly forgotten. *Perhaps there is something I can do.*

Dropping his hand, he looked out at the sleepy city. He had planned to fly until the ache in his chest eased, just for a few minutes before he returned and showed nothing but strength to the two people who needed him to protect and guide them.

But maybe he could do more than that.

The price would be steep. But he would pay it. *I would*

pay any price for Mark.

Taking to the air once more, knowing that time was of the essence, he shot across the city and flew with all the power in his wings. When he reached the woods, he kept going until he saw the place he must go. Lowering, he dropped just outside the cave.

Hesitating only a moment, he regarded a place he'd only heard spoken about in whispers, a place of death, sadness, and anger, a place anyone with any sense would avoid.

Striding forward, he ignored his racing heart. If it was the only way, then there was no use in hesitating, no use in rethinking the logic of his choice.

Because there's nothing logical about this.

It was dark inside, but the demon in him could see just fine. He wove deeper and deeper beneath the earth until his feet crunched onto bone. Staring down, he saw the path littered in the bones of different creatures—most human in form.

He had found the place.

Continuing forward, his heavy stone feet crunched more and more bones, but he remained in this form, knowing that to enter her domain as a human male would mean instant death. A light grew brighter ahead. He sensed the people waiting, knowing someone approached. As he drew closer to the entrance, he reached the light of the torches.

His stomach flipped. The stone walls were blackened, except where they were splattered with blood. Giant pillars of stone lifted the high ceiling of the cavern. Massive demons wearing armor made of bones lined the path, weapons at their side.

He moved down the path. None of the demons moved. But he didn't expect them to, not without *her* command.

At last, he broke out of the line of guards and drew

closer to the throne made of bones. She waited there for him, the Demon of Sacrifice. Her face was that of a young, beautiful woman with dark hair and eyes that were dark, with the slightest violet-shade. She wore a black dress that moved and flowed about her as if trying to pull free from the violent power that swelled from within her.

Crunching on yet more bones, he reached the steps before her throne and waited.

"Kneel," she ordered, and the word vibrated through the room.

Against his will, he collapsed onto his knees, staring up at her.

"You have made a mistake, gargoyle." Her words were like the tensing of a bow, drawing the air from the room. "I am the Demon of Sacrifice. I am the one who destroys men, those foul creatures who harm women and children. Any woman may come to me, and I will offer her my powers in exchange for vengeance."

Her head cocked to the side. "You are that most hated creature... man, in stone or flesh. I do *not* help men."

His throat tightened as she spoke, as if her very hands were closing around his throat. "I knew all this before I came. I even knew that you might kill me before you heard my words."

Something unreadable flashed in her eyes. "And yet, you came. Why?"

"It was worth the risk."

She crossed her long legs and the skirts moved yet again in their eerie, unnatural way. "Speak."

The tightness in his throat eased enough for him to speak. "We seek to overthrow Caine. My demon-brothers and I, along with our angel, have been searching out the true rulers of the realms, because Caine is corrupt. He is turning innocents into demons, and thugs into angels, and we plan to stop him."

The woman rose slowly, her eyes wide. "You're saying... not everyone who is a demon sinned so greatly that they deserved their punishment?"

He shook his head. "No."

To his amazement, the demon began to pace, her powers electric in the room. "I never imagined such a thing. I just thought that after what was done to me—that I held some blame—that I deserved—"

Her gaze snapped back to him, and for one horrible moment the pain and suffering in her eyes made the protective gargoyle within him want to roar in rage. Then, the look was gone. "I have never helped a man... except my brothers, but I will hear you out."

"Thank you," Tristan whispered. "It has been decreed that it will take all ten Immortals to overthrow Caine. They are the rightful rulers of the realms. My brother sacrificed his life to learn their whereabouts. He has told us that time is of the essence, and we cannot save him and them. I know that what I'm asking is a great thing and no simple task, but you are the only one who can help us. Can you prevent Caine from destroying Mark's soul while we save the world?"

Her brows rose. "You're asking me to go against the most powerful man in existence."

"I am."

"He will come after me for this."

"I know."

She studied him. "So, what makes you think I will help you?"

He tried to hide his unease. "I have been told that you

wish for one thing above all else, and even though I don't think it's what's best for you, I can give it to you."

A guarded look came over her face. "I want for nothing but vengeance against men."

"And a stone heart."

Shock registered on her face.

"You don't want to feel anything anymore. You want the human part of you to die."

She moved closer, her voice lowering. "I wish that more than anything, but I'm told such a thing is impossible."

"Not if a gargoyle gives you his essence, that which makes him a gargoyle."

Her hands came together before her, clenched above her heart. "Give it to me."

He shook his head. "My friend, Mark..."

She released her hands and went back to pacing. "I cannot prevent his soul from judgment..."

Tristan's hope fled.

"But I can buy you some time."

"How much?"

"Three days."

Tristan shook his head. "We need more than that."

She whirled on him. "That's all I can give. Take it or leave it."

His breathing became rapid. Was he really going to do this? Give up being a gargoyle forever?

"Alright, but you must allow me to remain a gargoyle until I've completed my task. I can't save the world with the flesh of a man."

She moved to stand in front of him and held out a delicate hand. "It's a deal."

Power swelled around her and magic swept over him in a wave of heat, suffocating in its terrible beauty.

He raised his hand, and she snatched it.

Black magic exploded from beneath them, dark shadows that lifted them into the air and swirled in a storm of chaos. He tried to tear his hand free, but her magic was too powerful. Something in her life had created a creature of such rage that it overtook her and made her into this demon, a demon more powerful than he ever imagined.

White light began to pull from him. It was uncomfortable at first, and then painful. A scream tore from his lips, and he fought against whatever was happening to him, but there was no escape.

At last, in front of him, a swirling light formed into a heart and pulsed with white light.

With her free hand, she cradled it in her palm.

They dropped to the floor. She came down gracefully onto her feet, while he fell onto his side in the sea of bones.

She whirled around, her black skirts flying about her. Seating herself back on her throne, she set the white, pulsing heart on the arm of her chair. The look on her face was one of complete satisfaction.

At last, he drew in a breath, coughing. The pain still held him in its grip, but he tried to breathe through it.

She smiled. "I never said it wouldn't be painful. Now, my gargoyle, you will attempt this task of yours. In three days' time, whether you succeed or fail, I will devour your stone essence, and you will be nothing more than a demon."

He struggled back onto his feet, rubbing at the ache in his chest. "Thank you."

She wasn't looking at him. She was looking at the pulsing heart.

Slipping from the room, he pushed himself faster, even though his body screamed in protest with each step. Now, Mark's soul would be safe. They had three days to find the

Immortals, and then, no matter what, they would wage their war on Caine.

urcy was so angry, angry and scared. Where the hell was Tristan? He'd told them they needed to hurry to save the Immortals. He'd told them that they couldn't help Mark.

And then? He'd disappeared.

"Surcy!"

She spun at the sound of Daniel's voice. He was kneeling over Mark's body, which still lay there wrapped in a blanket. A black smoke rose from Mark, and slowly, his body faded until it was gone.

Her throat tightened.

"We knew it would happen," he reminded her, his tone strangely robotic.

She nodded, unable to force the words past her lips. The bodies of demons and angels never remained in this world. They guessed it was Mark's druid powers that had allowed his body to stay for so long. She'd prayed she would have more time.

Somehow, losing his body felt like losing him yet again.

She walked on legs that trembled and knelt beside Daniel, taking his hand.

"That fucking druid," Daniel whispered, his words holding tears. "I loved that idiot. I loved his stupid plants and that smile of his. He had a damned good fucking attitude about everything. I—I didn't deserve him."

She wanted to hug him, but he rose and tore from the room, slamming the door behind him.

Reaching out, she stroked the blanket that had held Mark and counted to thirty. Wiping away tears, she walked across the room. Daniel had locked his door, but she twisted the handle, snapping it off. Pushing open the door she saw him by the window, lighter in hand.

"Give it to me," she ordered.

His face twisted. "It doesn't even matter anymore."

"It matters to me."

His eyes held unshed tears. "My fire... issue... is nothing compared to all this bullshit. Mark and Tristan are the ones that helped me get clean. You should have seen them in the demon-realms. Do you have any idea how much using fire would've helped us escape? But no, the little shits pinned me down and wouldn't let me touch it. They wouldn't let me use it. They knew it'd killed me once, and they wouldn't allow it to happen again.

"You have no idea how much I hated them for that." Then, the flame went out and his hand dropped. "And no idea how much I loved them. No one ever cared before." Tears slid down his cheeks. "No one gave a fuck if I killed myself, until them."

His shoulders shook and his face fell into his hands.

Surcy raced across the room, grabbed the lighter, and tossed it out the window. Her arms wrapped around him, and she held the big demon, the fire mage, as he fought harder than she'd ever seen a person fight, to keep his control.

"Let it out," she told him.

But he didn't. His shoulders continued to shake. He didn't seem to breathe. He just held himself stiffly, fighting back his need to cry.

"The reason you want your fire so badly is because it's easier than feeling, but nothing will truly help until you mourn losing him."

A shudder came over his body as he took a deep breath.

Raising his head from her shoulder, she saw the two tears that had tracked down his cheeks. "That's just it, isn't it? We all know that Caine's going to kill him the second his soul is reborn. We're all acting like there's still a chance, but he's never going to send him to the demon-realm. He's going to destroy him, isn't he?"

She didn't know what to say.

He was right.

"We have three days."

Her head jerked up and she saw Tristan in the doorway. He looked pale.

"What?" Daniel asked, wiping at his face.

"I bought us three days. Caine can't destroy his soul in that time."

"How?"

Tristan shook his head. "It doesn't matter. It's done."

Daniel walked across the room, and she imagined a million possibilities. She didn't expect it when he wrapped Tristan in a hug. It wasn't their awkward pat on the back either. It was a strong hug. Tristan held him fiercely, like a father. She could see the anger in his eyes, his need to protect the man who was fragile in ways most people couldn't see.

She swallowed around the lump in her throat and wiped at the stray tears tracking down her cheeks. Since she'd arrived, memory gone and lost in the confusion, her demons had done nothing but focus on her. There was something amazing about this moment, because she felt she was seeing into who they were before, a team who watched out for each other.

Daniel pulled back. "Okay then," he cleared his throat. "Time to find some Immortals."

She rose. Three days wasn't a lot of time. But for Mark, they'd do anything.

3

Caine was angry as hell. His angels had been unable to deal with Surcy and her demons. He wished, yet again, that the stupid Fate hadn't thrown herself into the Soul Destroyer to protect some useless human. Right now, he could use her guidance.

He had the remaining Immortals under his power in places the angel and her demons could never find. He had a choice. Destroy the Immortals' souls to ensure he would remain in power and never be overthrown, or kill the Immortals still under his control, have them reborn, and start all over again, breaking them down to take their magic.

He froze in his pace. Or, he could take the druid's necklace, find the Immortals stolen from him, and finish breaking them. *Because even though I've invaded Surcy's mind, magic has blocked out enough of the sanctuary's location that I'm unable to find it. Those bastard druids and their powers...*

Once he got them, he could make them pay... and finally take their powers. The Fate had told him the best way to crack the Immortals, and he knew they were so close.

Could he really throw all his hard work away now?

Only if I truly fear Surcy and her demons.

His nails tapped on the arm of his throne. No, it was time to stop fearing the Fate's warnings. He feared no one. He needed to find the druid and take his necklace. He needed to find the location of the sanctuary, and he needed to capture all of the Immortals, once and for all.

And take their power. Then, and only then, could he be certain to remain sole ruler forever.

Without paying much attention, he tossed one soul after another into the demon realm. None of the white wisps shone too brightly, and none looked human enough to be useful.

And then, one soul flashed into the room, blinding in its power.

Climbing to his feet, he pushed the other souls away and drew it to him. When the creature met his eyes, he realized it had been a demon.

For one second, he almost tossed it into the demon-realm, but he froze when he realized. This wasn't just any demon, it was one of Surcy's, the very druid he had been seeking.

"Well, well, what do we have here?"

Mark neither flinched nor looked worried. "Hello, Caine."

Interesting.

"After everything, why are you here? How did you die?"

Mark said nothing.

Caine smiled. "No matter. With you gone, your necklace is no longer protected. Finding it should be easy without your power hiding it. Once I have the necklace, the Immortals will finally be mine."

The demon looked sad. "Is power really worth all of this?"

His teeth gritted together. "Only someone who has never tasted power would say something so foolish. Now, say goodbye, Mark. You won't be coming back. Your soul will never be reborn again." He pointed to the Soul Destroyer. "Enjoy your fate."

The demon didn't scream or try to escape. He simply lowered his head as if he had accepted his fate.

Which Caine found utterly annoying.

Flicking the druid into the Soul Destroyer, he waited for his screams. But Mark's soul simply hovered above the black pit.

Caine frowned and tried again and again and again, but the demon remained.

"What is this?"

Mark lifted his head from where he was suspended in air. "How the hell should I know?"

Turning, Caine shouted for his guard. "Bring my witch!"

The angel leapt into action, racing from the room. Within minutes, he'd returned with the young woman slung over his shoulder. He tossed her to the ground and the prisoner groaned and lay on her side, filthy and stinking of the prisons.

Caine gritted his teeth together. "Why won't this soul be destroyed?"

The witch lifted a hand, her weak, trembling arm at odds with her great power.

"There's a spell that prevents him from leaving this world."

Caine felt his rage swell. Who in all the realms would dare to defy him in such a way?

"Who?" he asked, the question hanging in the air.

"The Demon of Sacrifice," she whispered.

His jaw clenched. That was yet another soul he should

have destroyed. She'd become too powerful, and apparently, foolish.

Looking at his guard, he glared. "Bring her to me."

Then, glancing back at Mark, he nearly lost all control. The idea of someone having the audacity to defy his plans and stop his punishment... but then he froze as an idea hit him.

Destroying Mark's soul was a delicious punishment, but perhaps there was a better one, a punishment that might even lead him to the Immortals even faster.

Settling back into his throne, he waved Mark's soul toward him and smiled.

For the first time, the druid looked nervous.

He should be.

4

Surcy and her demons stood at the edge of a large farm surrounded by woods. It reminded her of somewhere, but she couldn't quite place where. The sunlight bathed the entire place in a glow that warmed it like a painting, but something lingered underneath the beauty and peace of the place, a bad scent she couldn't quite place.

Mark's note had said that the farmer of these lands was an Immortal, but he believed himself to be nothing but a human. She didn't know whether this man had somehow managed to avoid Caine and his angels, but she was planning for trouble.

And she was sure she was right.

"So, what's the plan?" Daniel asked.

"We get him, fast." She tried to take a step forward, but Tristan grabbed her shoulder.

Staring back at him in confusion, she frowned. "What's wrong?"

"This can't be like the other times. We have to move faster—"

"I just said that!"

He held up a hand, and she closed her mouth. "We can't explain why we're here. We just need to grab him and go for the next Immortal."

"We have to bring him to the sanctuary first though—"

"There isn't time."

Her stomach twisted. "But if we get caught, we lose all of them."

"And if we aren't fast enough, we lose all of them anyway."

After a second, Daniel sighed. "I'm with Tristan. If we could teleport into the sanctuary, that'd be one thing, but we're going to have to spend hours walking back and forth beyond the barrier. That's time we don't have."

Surcy didn't like it, but their logic was sound. Every second they wasted was dangerous. Caine could decide with the flick of his wrist to destroy the souls of any Immortals in his control, and then all would be lost forever.

"Fine, let's go."

They started across the field, her hands itching to call for her soul-blade, to not enter an unknown territory weaponless, but she forced herself to just keep walking. To hope for the best.

Suddenly, two children darted out of the corn field, laughing. A boy and girl that had the same dark hair and dark eyes. They had to be twins.

The girl's gaze slowly moved to them, and the laughter died on her face. She grabbed her brother's arm, the boy looked at them, and then they were tearing through the field away from them.

"What do we do?" Daniel asked. "Chase them?"

Tristan's deep voice came, soft and certain. "Never chase

children. There is nothing more fierce than a parent who thinks his child is in danger."

They continued forward, and seconds later, a farmer emerged from the cornfield. He gripped a pitchfork in one hand, like a stereotype. But other than that, he wasn't what she expected. For one, he seemed young, perhaps in his forties, with dark hair and a muscular body. And something in his stance—it screamed that he was ready for a fight.

"This isn't good," Daniel whispered.

"Just stay calm," Tristan said, his gaze locked on the man ahead of him.

They continued forward until they were about fifteen feet from him, then they stopped, trying their hardest to look non-threatening. The farmer's gaze ran over each of them for a minute, and she saw his jaw lock.

"What can I do for you three?"

"We have need of your help." Tristan's words were carefully chosen and screaming of caution.

"What sort of help?"

In the field behind him, white-winged angels appeared. Surcy took a step back, her fingers itching to call her blade. The six angels were dressed in the clothes of hard-working farmers, and their glamours made them appear human.

Are they working for the farmer?

She racked her brain, trying to figure out why. With each Immortal they had found, Caine had trapped them in their own personal hell. He planned to break them down slowly until he could finally steal their powers and become the most powerful being in existence.

So what hell were these angels creating for the farmer by working for him?

Tristan didn't react to the angels, never moving his eyes from the farmer. "Our car broke down on the road."

Some of the suspicion died from the farmer's tanned-face. "What's wrong with it?"

"The battery."

He regarded the three of them for a few more seconds. "I can jump you; just give me a minute to get my car."

One of the angels came up behind the farmer and patted his shoulder. "Don't worry, Clarence, we'll stay here and keep an eye on the wife and kids."

The farmer nodded. "Thanks."

She clenched her fists. Clarence might not understand what the angel meant, but she and her demons knew. The angels were threatening them. If they took off with Clarence, his wife and kids would pay.

Now what?

"Actually," Surcy rushed out. "I'm feeling a bit over-heated from the sun and walking so far. Would you mind if I get a glass of water?"

The farmer stared at her.

Think, Surcy, think!

She forced a smile. "Some women get morning sickness. Not me! I stay sick all day."

His gaze moved to her belly and he relaxed a little bit more. "My wife was the same way. Come on, then, I'm sure she'd be glad for the company."

The angel walked beside the farmer, explaining to him some problem with the chickens. She and her demons followed slowly behind, tense as they felt the other angels sliding through the cornfield, keeping pace with them. Their odds were a hell of a lot worse without Mark.

Before, we had a chance against all these angels, but now? Not at all.

Her eyes stung, and she was glad she didn't have to talk,

because she thought she'd start crying if she did, which was stupid as hell. She was supposed to be alert and ready for anything, but instead, her mind kept slipping back to Mark.

If she couldn't focus, she might make a mistake. She couldn't make a single mistake, not with the stakes this high.

By the time they walked past the broken down farm equipment and fenced-in animals, she was feeling less emotional, but even more nervous. Glancing behind her, she saw the angels glaring near the farm equipment.

Creepy fuckers.

The farmer went into the house and came back out a minute later, a woman and two children behind him. His wife was tall and thin, with long blonde hair, and bright blue eyes. She wore a smart-looking blouse and ironed slacks. When her gaze met Surcy's, she smiled.

"Welcome, I'm Beth. You want to join me inside for coffee while the boys jump-start your car?"

"Surcy," Daniel was suddenly at Surcy's side, his grip tight on her arm. "We shouldn't split up."

I know I agreed this would be fast, just in and out, but I can't leave this woman and her children behind. I just can't. I'm sorry.

She plastered on a smile. "Let go and act normal."

He released her arm, but she could sense his frustration.

"That sounds just perfect!" She moved up the porch, nodding at the farmer, and coming to stand beside his wife.

"We'll see you soon!" she called, waving to her demons.

Both men looked like they'd swallowed glass, but Tristan nodded in a casual way she knew was forced.

The farmer and her demons squeezed into his truck together, and Surcy looked back at them as she followed the woman into her house. Five angels used a glamour to conceal themselves, stretched their wings, and took off into the air. But a few angels remained, staring directly at her, a challenge in their gazes.

Swallowing hard, she closed the door behind her. *Now what?*

5

In the kitchen, Surcy sat at the little table. The house could only be described as a disaster. Toys and clothes were thrown everywhere, yogurt dripped off one wall, and pencils were stuck in the ceiling. Surcy glanced around the kitchen and out into the living room in shock.

"No kids yet?" Beth asked, smiling.

Surcy felt her cheeks blush and looked at the two little ones who had dragged coloring books onto the cluttered table beside her. "No, not yet."

"But Clarence said you were pregnant."

Surcy nodded.

"Then, just you wait, all this chaos... it's perfectly normal."

Something twisted in her heart. Being an angel meant she'd never have children, and she'd never had any in her human life either. For the first time, that seemed strangely sad.

"I never thought I'd have children," Surcy admitted softly, her gaze constantly sliding around the house, looking for danger.

The woman laughed, putting ground coffee beans into a fancy looking coffee-maker. "Why not?"

Surcy shrugged. "I guess... I thought I wouldn't have the chance."

Beth nodded, as if that made perfect sense. "It was kind of an adjustment for me. I work in marketing, so I didn't want to give up the money, the perks, or my freedom."

"But it was all worth it."

The woman laughed. "Well, it isn't easy. In fact, it's the hardest thing I've ever done in my life, but I wouldn't change it for the world."

Her gaze slid over the chaos again. *Is this really what being a parent is all about?*

The little girl rose from her seat and carried a picture to her mom. "I drew our family."

The mom knelt down and swooned over the messy drawing. Which pretty much made Surcy's heart melt.

And then the girl pointed out some of the people tucked away in the field. "And those are the bad men."

Her mom stiffened. "Sunshine, we've talked about this..."

"They bring death and destruction everywhere they go." The girl's voice held absolute certainty.

The boy rose from his seat and moved to the window. A little potted plant was brown and bent in the shadows of the windowsill. He grabbed the pot and looked at Surcy, holding her gaze. She frowned as he touched the little leaf very deliberately, and suddenly, the plant rose tall and green.

Whoa!

"Forest!" His mother's voice sounded panicked.

The woman hurried over and plucked the plant out of his hand, setting it on the windowsill. The boy didn't look the least bit concerned. Instead, he was watching Surcy closely. His mother? She whirled on Surcy, pulling the boy closer, panic in her gaze.

Just calm her down. "Uh, sorry, what did you guys say? I was kind of lost in my own thoughts."

The mother's shoulders relaxed. "It's just... Forest and his sister are special. And, it's hard to parent children who are... unique."

Surcy nodded. "I can't even imagine."

"And the bad men make sure nothing gets better around here," the girl said.

Her mother started to say something, but Surcy cut her off. "Who are the bad men?"

"The farmers daddy hired," she explained. "They're here to hurt us."

Beth laughed awkwardly. "Kids have such wild imaginations."

Fuck it.

"Actually, I think she's right."

The mom froze. "Wh—what do you mean?"

Just do it!

"The men I came here with... we're not here about a car. We're here because all of you are in danger. Your husband is special. Powerful. And apparently, your kids have some of his powers too."

"No," Beth interrupted. "He isn't like them."

"He is. He just doesn't know it yet."

Silence enveloped them.

"We're here to take you all someplace safe. Some place they can't hurt you."

The woman shook her head. "This is our home."

"I don't know why Caine hasn't ordered them to kill all of you yet, but it's only a matter of time."

The woman pulled her children closer. "I don't know who you are, but I think you need to go."

"She's telling the truth," the boy said. "Caine probably wanted to see if Sunshine and I had powers too, which is why we've been so careful around them. But now that the demons have come, the angels won't risk losing us."

The mom looked pale. "Honey, who is Caine?"

He glanced up slowly. "He's the man who kills daddy over and over again."

She looked like she was going to be sick. "And the demons?"

"The men she came with," he said, pointing to Surcy.

"Stop," the mother said. "None of this can be true."

Surcy rose slowly. "My men and your husband are going to reach the road any minute, and once they do, there's going to be a fight. The angels they left behind, the bad men, they're going to attack us."

"Mommy, I know you're scared, but you don't need to be," Sunshine told her mom.

Surcy moved closer. She needed to take their hands. She needed to teleport them free.

The mother took a step back, clinging to her children.

And then, the door was kicked down, the sound like lightning cracking through the silence. The mom looked to the door. The white-winged angels held out their flaming blue soul-blades.

Surcy leapt forward, grabbed the kids, and willed herself to teleport them all away. She heard the sound of a sword whizzing past, and then someone screaming, before the sound was torn away. Teleporting was harder with so many people, and she was working to erase their teleportation path at the same time. By the time they appeared near the road, she was breathing hard.

"Mom?" The little boy's voice came soft and scared.

Surcy turned... the mom had a soul-blade pierced through her chest. The children held onto each of her arms as she sagged between them. Surcy knelt down, heart racing. What could she do?

And then, the soul-blade vanished and blood poured from her wound.

"We need to—need to." But the words wouldn't leave her lips.

What can I do?

And then, she had an idea. It might not save the woman, but it would give her a chance.

"Can you stay here?" she asked the children.

The woman's eyes were closed, and her skin was pale, but her chest rose and fell.

"Why?" the girl asked, her voice shaking.

"I'm going to take your mom to get help."

The girl nodded and took her brother's hand. Surcy pulled the mother into her arms, looked back at the two frightened children one more time, and teleported away.

She appeared in the middle of the hospital in their town. It was a place she'd been a few times before and could remember well enough to reach.

A nurse glanced up from behind a desk, and her eyes widened.

"She was stabbed!"

Instantly, the nurse grabbed a bed and wheeled it closer. Surcy laid the woman down, staring at her face, praying that the mother would live.

The nurse shouted for a doctor.

With regret swimming in her stomach, Surcy teleported away.

Materializing back by the side of the road, Survey

opened her mouth to tell the children the next step, but they were gone. On the ground? She spotted white feathers.

Surcy ran down the road, searching for any sign of the children. When she spotted people up ahead, hope blossomed in her heart, but it was only Daniel and Tristan with the farmer.

As she drew closer, she saw four angels dead at their feet. Daniel's arm bled, but Tristan wore his gargoyle form, a sword in hand.

The farmer stood between them, holding a dagger of his own. Within seconds, the bodies of the angels disappeared in a flash of light.

At her approach, all of them looked at her.

"Are you hurt?" Tristan asked, stepping forward.

Surcy looked down at the blood covering her jeans and t-shirt. Beth's blood.

She shook her head, slowly.

Tristan's emotions disappeared, hidden behind a mask of indifference.

"Then, whose blood is it?" Daniel asked.

A second later, she saw it hit him.

"Where's my family?" the farmer asked, tension in his voice.

Her entire chest ached. How could she tell him his children had been stolen and his wife was hurt—perhaps dead? She was supposed to keep them safe, and she'd failed in every way.

"We need to get you out of here," Tristan said, unsettlingly calm.

The farmer stepped back from them. "You said you came here to save us, so why would we leave without them?"

Daniel whirled on him. "We came here to save you. *You're* the important one. We wanted to save them too, but if we couldn't—"

"Not a fucking chance!" Clarence snarled. "I'm not going anywhere without them."

Surcy struggled to form her explanation. "One of the angels wounded your wife. I teleported her to a hospital."

"And the kids?" he asked, taking a step closer.

"They—they got them."

"You mean the bloodthirsty creatures who wanted to kill me have my children?"

She nodded.

"*Where*?"

"I don't know."

He stared at her for one horrible minute that seemed to last a lifetime. "If they wanted me, they wouldn't have gone far. I bet they're back at the farm."

Her stomach twisted. He was probably right.

"You can't go back," Tristan told him. "They've had time to gather their forces. We'd have no chance."

"I don't care."

Tristan gave her a nod, so subtle the others didn't see it.

He wants me to teleport away with him? I can't just do that to him. I can't leave the kids here.

She shook her head. "We need to save the kids."

Tristan's gaze met hers. "The fate of this world rests on getting all ten Immortals. If a single one dies, we have failed."

"Tristan..."

"Take us out of here." He spoke the words in staccato, one after the other, anger and frustration embedded in each one.

Her gut clenched, but she realized that he was right. They couldn't risk the Immortal. The angels would be waiting to attack. They only had one option.

She took their hands. Tristan grabbed the farmer. Before he could protest, she teleported them away, leaving the children behind.

7

Surcy teleported them to the top of a building, in a city she'd never been to, but that Mark had described in his note. Instantly, the farmer sagged to his knees, his mouth dropped in shock.

"The next Immortal is here," she said, pulling out Mark's note from her pocket and handing it to Daniel.

"Where the hell are we?" The farmer shouted. "Where are my kids?"

She looked at her demons, memorizing their faces, her heart in her throat. They were everything to her, everything in this world.

But she couldn't let those children die.

"Don't worry," she told Clarence. "I'll do everything I can to save them."

Tristan's brows drew together.

And, she teleported away.

Heart hammering, she stood in the cornfield just outside the farmhouse. Slowly moving forward she crept closer, gently pushing aside stalks with each step. Everything was far too quiet. Even the wind hardly stirred, and on the air she smelled the plants, the sun, and the sky, like all of it was alive and open to her. Underneath it all, the scent of copper lingered, the mother's blood still wet and sticky on her clothes.

Up ahead, she heard a child crying. It took everything in her not to sprint forward. If she got killed, it wouldn't help the children get back to their father.

When she reached the edge of the field, she froze, squinting through the leaves of the corn. Inching a little forward, she held back a gasp. No less than fifty angels stood in perfect formation in front of the little house.

On the porch? The children stood before Frink. He clutched them against his chest and held his glowing blade at their throats.

Her heart sank. The blue flames just barely licked at their flesh, but she could see they were in pain and scared.

There was only one way she could think to save them. If she failed, they would all die.

Closing her eyes, she counted to three, feeling sweat run down her back. Feeling how her legs trembled.

"Surcy, let's stop these games," Frink said, his voice wasn't loud, but it carried in the stillness. "Why keep pretending you can be anything but an angel? None of us can choose. We are what Caine assigns us to be, and you are his soldier."

She said nothing, just watched the blade at the children's throat. It needed to move, just an inch or two away. That's all she needed.

Frink laughed. "You know what the best part of all of this is? You truly don't know that you're still working for us."

If she could tune his words out, she would. Instead she sat, waiting for the opportunity to strike, unable to escape his cruel words.

"Did you really think a man as powerful as Caine couldn't reach you? That your little garden house and three weak demons could keep him away? Think about it, Surcy, ask yourself why you're still alive."

She refused to think about it. Frink hated her with a passion. He was trying to distract her, trying to get inside her brain.

"Because, and this is just so delicious, you're his little spy."

The words fell like stones in her belly. Of course Frink would lie about something so terrible. He wanted to hurt her. To make her doubt herself.

"The man who can affect memories... it's just pure fun, right? He can sneak into your room late at night, pull your memories from your mind, and leave without you even knowing he was there. He could find out all that you and your demons had done. And he could discover where you were keeping the Immortals."

Nightmares came back to her, of Caine standing over her bed, of him pressing pain into her mind.

She wanted his words to be a lie, but they felt true.

Metal touched her throat. Her thoughts died away as she realized that a soul-blade threatened her. The angel behind her spoke in a low voice. "You shouldn't have come here."

A woman angel, then. Sometimes they were the most vicious. Surcy kept still and waited. She waited to lose her head, to be killed and returned to Caine with the knowledge that she'd failed these children, but nothing happened.

The woman's voice came again, louder this time. "All of you rebels are the same, so certain you can defeat Caine and all his angels. I seriously don't understand where you get your reckless faith." She paused for a second. The voice lowered, just for Surcy. "Listen, I still don't know what I believe, but I don't believe in Caine. I won't directly help you. I won't put my own life at risk. But I can distract them."

Her heart raced, filling her ears. She wanted to ask the angel why. Why would she help their cause?

But then, the blade was gone.

A second later, an angel stood in front of the ranks of soldiers. Her blonde hair fell down her back, and she wore a pale dress. "I saw them. The demons and farmer are trying to sneak through the back woods."

Frink's blade slipped slightly further from the children's throats. "Alright, here's the plan—"

Surcy called her soul-blade into her hand and teleported. Appearing just behind Frink, she sliced off his head, for what felt like the millionth time. Her arms wrapped around the children as his body fell between them, and she teleported away, erasing their path behind her.

When they reached just outside of the sanctuary, she sent her blade away.

The children turned to her, tears in their eyes.

"Where's mom and dad?" the girl asked.

Her heart lurched. "Your mom is in a hospital. Your dad is helping to defeat the bad men."

Tears tracked down their cheeks, and the boy touched his raw-looking throat. "What do we do now?"

She nibbled her lip. "Through these woods is a sanctuary of magic. Protected so that the angels can't reach it. There are people like your father and you there. You'll be safe. I could take you, but I think your dad and my demons need me."

They stared at her for a long minute, and then took each other's hands in a movement she knew gave them comfort.

"Just tell us which way to go," the girl said.

The boy nodded. "My plants will help me find the way."

Surcy hesitated only a moment and then pointed, praying that she was doing the right thing. The children gave her one last look, then turned and walked in the right direction. With each step, the plants bent to the side, making an easy path.

Please, please stay safe.

Taking a deep breath, she teleported away.

8

D aniel squared off with the farmer, his fists clenched in rage. "You're going to do what we say or—"

"I won't do a damned thing without my wife and children!" Clarence shouted, advancing on him.

Fuck this. As much as I want to punch him, there's an easier way.

His fists unclenched. "They're safe," he whispered. Demon magic flowed through the words, and the effect of them was almost instant.

The anger drained from the farmer's face. "Where?"

That's right. Believe me. Do as I ask.

"Surcy has gone back for them. She'll put them somewhere no one can hurt them."

It took everything inside of Daniel to use his natural demon-ability to convince the farmer, because the truth was he was on the verge of something terrible. Surcy had dropped them on this fucking building and gone back to face unimaginable danger. And why? For a couple kids they didn't know.

3838

3838

38

In his mind, he pictured the little boy and girl, and his stomach clenched. The angels would have no use for them as anything but pawns in their games. If no one came back for them...

He shuddered, imagining them lying bloodied and dead on the ground.

But still... either they all should have gone back or none of them. Tristan and Surcy might value the Immortals more than themselves, but if they lost Surcy, did he even care about Caine?

Maybe. A little.

"I want to see them," the farmer said, and a little anger returned to his eyes.

Tristan took a step closer. "There is no more time for this. Clarence, did you see those creatures? Those angels who attacked us?"

The farmer nodded.

"Those creatures were disguising themselves as your farmhands to be close to you. They were waiting for a signal from a being known as Caine, The Judge of all living beings. And once they were given the signal, they were instructed to kill you and your family."

His eyes widened. "Why?"

Tristan titled his head, in a very gargoyle-like way. "Because you are one of only ten beings powerful enough to stop Caine and his angels."

Clarence began to shake his head. "I'm not—"

"You are. And if we don't move quickly enough, Caine will win this war, and you and your family will never be safe again."

The farmer studied him. "Do I have your word that my family is safe?"

Fuck. The damn gargoyle won't lie.

"Yes," Daniel rushed out. "They're safe. We just need to hurry and find the rest of your kind, so we can stop that murderous bastard."

The man exhaled loudly, and his hand shook as he ran fingers through his hair. "If I wasn't just attacked by fucking angels... if I wasn't here talking to a gargoyle and whatever the hell you are... I'd think you were both nuts. But, if my family is safe, and this stops them from being hurt again, I'll go with you."

Daniel hadn't realized how worried he'd been that the guy would just keep refusing to help them until that moment. And while the farmer's acceptance eased some of his fears, nothing would calm him until he saw Surcy again.

"So," he turned to Tristan, "who are we looking for next?"

The gargoyle opened the paper and stared, frowning. "I thought we'd agreed to find the God of Sin next, but this place isn't right." He stared for a minute longer. "She brought us to the other Immortal first. The Goddess of Life."

Daniel shrugged. "I guess she made a mistake."

Tristan frowned down at the paper. "Perhaps."

"Tick tock."

Tristan looked at him and raised a brow. "Helpful."

As they found the roof exit and climbed down the stairs, Daniel almost smiled. It wasn't often the gargoyle was sarcastic. Hopefully that meant he wasn't too worried about Surcy. The idea immediately calmed him. If Tristan, Mr. Natural Protector himself, was feeling confident, that meant Daniel should be too.

A weight lifted from his shoulders.

They moved through the town and continued walking,

occasionally checking the address. Tristan could fly them there, but without knowing the area, travel by ground was easier.

To Daniel's annoyance, the farmer peppered him with questions. Every. Single. Step of the way.

"What am I?"

"The God of Earth."

"What does that mean?"

"You have powers."

"How come I haven't seen any before? Now my kids have some special abilities, but I've never noticed anything."

"Caine wiped your memories."

And on and on. When they reached the quiet suburban neighborhood, Daniel was ready to punch the shit out of the human. Normally, he didn't care, but they had things to do, bigger things than answering questions.

Maybe they should have dropped him at the sanctuary.

They reached the house, but it looked empty.

"So what now?" Daniel asked, not bothering to hide his annoyance.

Tristan opened his mouth, but a woman spoke instead.

"If you're looking for the Carters, they won't be home for a little while."

Daniel spun around to see woman sitting on the porch next door. She was perhaps in her mind-forties and lovely in a quiet way. Her hair was in a messy bun on her head, she wore pajamas that said, "best mom ever," and she didn't have a drop of makeup on.

In other words, she was the kind of woman that any smart man would love.

"Hi," Daniel greeted her, turning on his most charming smile and moving closer.

A blush darkened her cheeks. "Hi... uh, are you friends of the Carters?"

"College friends of her hubs," he lied, hoping he'd made a good guess.

She set her coffee on her knee. "Oh, are you guys doctors too?"

He nodded. "The best in L.A. But we haven't seen him in a while. We thought we'd drop in and surprise him."

She stared down at her drink. "I'm sure Richard would love that, but he's at a conference this weekend. It's just Nichole."

Well, that will make this lie easier.

"Oh, that's too bad. Well, I guess at least we can visit with her. We've never actually met her."

Her gaze swung back up to them. "Oh, you'll love Nichole. She's beautiful and smart and funny." She sipped her drink and mumbled. "Not that Richard notices."

Daniel's ears perked up. "Would it be okay if we hung out with you just a few minutes? If she doesn't come home, I guess we can try another time. We were just stopping by between flights, so we really hoped to see them and see their house. You know? Catch up."

She patted her hair, looking flustered. "Uh, sure."

Moving closer, he sat down on the porch steps next to her and leaned back, stretching his legs out. "So, tell us about Nichole. What does she do?"

"Well, uh, nothing right now. She stopped teaching when they decided to start having kids."

He smiled. "Well, having kids is like having three jobs, so it makes sense."

She laughed, shyly. "Yeah, if only they didn't have infertility issues, I think it would've been wonderful."

Oops.

"Richard mentioned something about that."

She rolled her eyes. "I'm sure he did. And I'm sure he just *happened* to mention that the issues are her fault. And he just *happened* to mention that she's done IVF unsuccessfully ten times now, and how hard that's been on *him*."

Daniel's heartbeat sped up. "You don't sound like you like him much."

She immediately hid her anger behind a mask. "I didn't say that."

Sighing, he rolled his neck. *Demon-abilities, take two.* "You can be honest with us. We know what an ass he can be sometimes."

Instantly, she relaxed, but the effect was deeper on her than it had been on the farmer. Her eyes grew a little glassy, like she'd had one too many drinks. "Richard is the biggest dick in the world. We've been trying to convince her to leave him for years. I mean, he's a fucking doctor. They aren't hurting for money, but he gives her a god-damn allowance, like a child. I don't mean a budget. I mean her name isn't on any of the accounts. He gives her money and tells her that's all she gets for food and gas. The woman hasn't bought new clothes in years. She can never go out because she doesn't have any money to do it."

Daniel raised a brow. "Wow."

"It's fucking financial abuse!" She glared at all the men. "And then he tells her who she can and cannot speak to, who she can and cannot be friends with. She can't talk to her family anymore, or most of her friends. He doesn't even like me talking to her, but he can't stop me, the asshole."

"That's... controlling."

She nodded, looking like she wanted to shout *yes*! "But if all of that wasn't bad enough, there's the infertility stuff. He makes her feel like garbage just because she can't have kids.

I mean, she's broken-hearted over it. She volunteers at a hospital, helping to take care of the babies in the NICU. She lavishes them with care, and they get so big and healthy. She's... like a miracle worker. But then, she can't have her own kids. Can you imagine the torture she must experience every day?"

The Goddess of Life can't have kids. Caine, you're a fucking monster.

"It would be pure torture." Daniel looked up and met Tristan's gaze, and he knew they were both thinking the same thing.

He watched as a car slowed and pulled into the Carter's driveway.

Daniel turned to the woman and smiled. "It looks like she's home. Thanks for talking with us."

The woman nodded, her mouth twisting in disappointment. "No problem."

Unable to walk away leaving the woman unhappy, he leaned closer. "I know this isn't appropriate, but if I was single, well, you're just my type."

It was like sunshine blossomed behind her face. "Yeah, you into women who are complete disasters?"

"Nah, I'm into women who are naturally stunning." He winked and rose.

Was he attracted to her? No, Surcy was it for him. She was the sun and the moon, and the only person he could ever want like that. But he'd known a lot of heartache and loneliness in his life, and this woman screamed of loneliness. She practically vibrated with a sense of worthlessness, and it broke his heart. No one should ever feel that way about themselves.

He looked back one last time at her star-struck expression and glanced at the stoic gargoyle and the farmer.

Clarence looked confused as hell, but Tristan gave a sharp nod. His friend knew exactly what he was doing, and even though Tristan didn't hit on women to brighten their days, he didn't disapprove of what Daniel did either. Tristan knew Daniel's weakness for lost souls.

9

Tristan, Daniel, and Clarence moved to the Carter's driveway as the woman climbed out of her car. To his surprise, she was young, perhaps her early twenties. Her long blonde hair was pulled back into a neat ponytail, a pink sweater that looked worn, and white capri pants. When she closed her door, she turned around, looked at them, jumped slightly, and gave a nervous laugh.

"Sorry. I didn't see you there."

He gave a warm smile. "We're friends of Richard's. We came to visit with him between flights."

A guarded look came over her face. "He went to a conference."

"Oh," he glanced at the farmer and Tristan. "That's disappointing. He's always talking about his beautiful wife and home. We thought we'd finally get a chance to meet you and see a little about his life after college."

She picked nervously at the sleeve of her jacket. "Richard doesn't like me around men without him."

Daniel had to work like hell to keep his anger from

showing. She looked terrified. No real man would scare a woman like this.

"I'm sure he wouldn't mind the three of us, right?" he asked, using his demon-abilities.

Some of the nervousness left her expression. "I guess. Come in then. I can make coffee."

They followed her inside, but not before Daniel paused at the door to look around. Why were there no angels guarding her?

He has to be the one creating this torture for the Goddess of Life, right? Or does he have nothing to do with it?

They walked through an immaculately clean home and to the little table inside a big kitchen. She immediately put a kettle on the stove, switching the flame on. He swallowed hard, pulling his gaze from the fire. It called to him, coaxing him to connect with it, just a little.

Focus! "Nichole?"

The woman startled again, a reflex like an animal of prey. "Yes? Did you—did you need—I forgot snacks. Gosh, I'm so dumb. I'll get them."

Daniel rose from his chair, the wood legs scraping against the tile. "No, please, sit down."

She shook her head and went to the fridge. "Richard always says how rude I can be. I'll make a plate of cheese and—"

He had crossed the room without thinking and took her wrist. "Richard is an asshole. You don't need to wait on us like a servant."

Her eyes widened, but she said nothing.

We need to get her out of here, but if we can do it without freaking the hell out of her, we should.

Especially since we can't just teleport away with her now.

"Have you ever felt like you didn't belong in this world? Like it fit like a bad outfit."

He didn't know what he expected. Denial. Fear. Uncertainty.

But instead, she whispered. "Yes. Every moment."

His heart clenched. "Well, that's because you don't belong here. You're a goddess, Nichole. A creature meant for bigger and better things than a loveless marriage and a life without happiness."

She stared. "I don't... I don't understand."

He took a deep breath, knowing he was taking a risk. "Ever read any books about magic and other worlds?"

She nodded.

"Well, all of that exists."

Her brows drew together. "I'm sorry, but is this a joke?"

"No," he denied quickly.

"Because this feels like something Richard would do. All of this actually does. The last time I talked with a friendly man, Richard had paid him to do it, to show what a slut I am."

"Holy fuck," Daniel muttered, before he could stop himself. "No, we aren't being paid by Richard to torture you. Actually, how would you like to never have to be around that asshole again?"

Tears sparkled in her eyes. "I can never escape him."

He released her wrist. "Yes, you can. And we're here to set you free. Come with us, Nichole."

"Where?"

Tristan rose behind them, the chair scraping loudly against the floor. "To a world outside of this one. Where I'm a gargoyle and you are a goddess."

With his last spoken word, he shifted. His skin turned grey and wings grew from his back.

She shot away, her back hitting the fridge behind her. "You're—you're..."

The farmer spoke. "I just found out about all this nutty stuff too, but it's true. You aren't going crazy or anything like that, but we need to leave, and fast. The bad guys that came after me might be here too."

She stared at all of them for a long moment. "So, you're here to take me away from Richard, to a world with magic. Where I'm a goddess?"

They all nodded.

She closed her eyes, took a deep breath, and clenched her hands. "Okay, let's go."

Wow, that was easy.

Together they moved through the house and back toward the front door. Without Surcy to teleport them, it'd be difficult to get to where they needed to go. But Tristan could take them.

Then, the door opened.

They all froze.

A man stood in the door with short, white hair and pale silver eyes. From his back, red wings sprouted.

"Richard," she said, her voice shaking. "You're home early."

His mouth curled into a sick smile. "And where do you think you're going?"

For a minute he wondered, did the angel know what they were? Did he know why they were there? And then, he remembered that Tristan no longer wore his glamour.

This creature knew exactly what was going on.

Tristan moved so that he stood in front of them. "An arch-angel... I thought Caine did away with your kind. I thought he didn't like any other beings to have that kind of power."

The angel's sickening smile widened. "Well, you were wrong." He lifted his hand, pointed it at Tristan, and the gargoyle exploded raining down dust on all of them.

Coughing, Daniel's heart racing. *What the fuck just happened? Tristan? Tristan!*

No, it couldn't have happened. Tristan was a gargoyle! No one was powerful enough to destroy him so easily!

The dust settled, and there, inches from him, the archangel stood. And Tristan? He was gone, leaving behind nothing but a pile of dust and stone.

"What did you do to him?" Daniel's voice shook with rage.

The creature smirked. "The same thing I'm going to do to you. But raining demon-flesh is a little messier."

"Run!" he shouted to the Immortals.

The farmer didn't need to be told twice. He grabbed the woman's arm, and they raced for the back door.

"How... cute. You think they'll escape me."

Daniel moved backwards, one slow step at a time. His mind racing. How could he save the Immortals? How could he stop this being?

And then, the little flame beneath the kettle came into his view. And he knew.

Gesturing slightly with his hand, he called the flame. It jumped from the stove to the counters, cabinets and floor, it leapt to the little curtain on the window above the sink and began to devour it all. Energy coursed through Daniel, and power.

The angel saw none of it, his gaze focused on Daniel. "You've made such a terrible mistake, thinking you could overpower Caine. Instead, you brought another Immortal straight into our hands."

Daniel swallowed hard, trying not to look back at the

flames. "They were guarded this whole time. Nothing has changed."

He drew back his lips, revealing sharp teeth. "Everything has changed. Caine has decreed that the last of the Immortals in our care will be brought to him. No more games. And... and this is the best part. He's decided that your lives are forfeit. At last."

"Nothing was stopping him from killing us before."

The angel cocked its head. "Do you know why Caine doesn't like arch-angels? Because to create us, he must link himself to us. That means we can read pieces of his thoughts. We can sense some of his emotions. And do you know what I'm sure of?"

Smoke was beginning to rise, and the kitchen was nearly consumed. *How has the angel not sensed it?*

"The Fate told him that upon your deaths, he would lose the war against the Immortals. But when your little friend, Mark, died, he realized something. You didn't have to stay dead. And there's a way to ensure your use to him."

Sweat poured down Daniel's face and his arms. The fire moved out of the kitchen and into the living room, smoke billowing, filling the room.

At last, the angel looked at it, then back at him. "Oh, how delightful. You thought to kill me with your fire."

Suddenly, the angel disappeared.

Daniel looked around, heart racing, but the angel was nowhere to be seen.

Turning, he raced for the backdoor, but when he pulled on the handle, it wouldn't open. On the other side of the door, the archangel smiled. His words came as clearly as if he was standing beside Daniel, whispering in his ear.

"You remember how painful it was to die by fire, fire-mage? How about angel-fire?"

Turning, he watched as the orange flames turned to blue. *No!* He had no control over that type of fire. It was too hot and too powerful.

The room grew painfully warm. The black smoke billowed, darker and heavier, consuming the oxygen.

Daniel turned back to the glass door and threw himself at it, but it held. Over and over again he tried to break the glass, but then he saw the glass, sparkling against the light of the angel-fire. And he knew. It had been enchanted.

The fire was everywhere now, sealing him into the living room.

There was nowhere to go.

Moving closer to the flames, he knelt down where the dust from Tristan lay. He picked it up in one of his hands, and sat, closing his eyes. This would not be a quick death. It would be slow and horrible.

But at least he still had Tristan.

And maybe the Immortals might even escape.

At the window, he sensed the archangel, drinking in the sight of what would soon happen.

But his enemies didn't matter, only Surcy, Tristan, and Mark mattered. At least in death he would be reunited with them. Even if only for a short time before Caine destroyed their souls.

10

Surcy teleported to the other side of the world. It was night there, and the city below her was massive. The lights so bright in contrast with the darkness that it hurt her eyes. People were everywhere. Walking. Crammed onto the crowded streets in cars that barely moved in the traffic.

Somewhere in this chaos, the God of Sin hid.

If she could find him quickly enough, she could teleport back to her demons and the Immortals. They would all be safe, and they could hurry to save Mark in time, before Caine destroyed his soul. She'd known her demons would never let her pursue an Immortal alone. So, she'd done it without telling them.

They'd forgive her when they saw that it was the only way.

She teleported from the rooftop to the street. Walking slowly, she looked for the building Mark had described in his note. Neon signs flashed at her from every direction. Men and women made her offers, selling their bodies for a price.

Her skin crawled. This was a terrible place. Truly, a place not of sins, but of heartache. No one chose this life... it was thrust upon them.

Crossing the street, she froze as she spotted the little building wedged between two others. The neon sign said, "Sin," in bold red letters. *Of course it did.*

A car honked at her. She stiffened, realizing that the light had changed. Sprinting across the road, she made it to the other crosswalk and to the side of the street with the building.

When she reached the door, painted the deepest shade of black, she knocked. A massive man opened the door and stared down at her frowning.

She hesitated. "I'd like to come in."

He said nothing. Did he understand English?

Sighing, she realized she didn't have time for this. Glancing around his shoulder, she saw a room bathed in red lights. He shifted to block her view, but it was enough.

Closing her eyes, she teleported inside.

Standing in the center of the room, she saw that it was empty. A dark staircase led deeper beneath the ground. Hurrying from the room before she could be spotted by the guard, she rushed down the staircase and into another room bathed in red.

In the center of the back wall, a man lay on a massive bed tangled with women. And lining the sides of the room? Angels with glamours had sex with one, or more, partners in what she could only describe as a drug or alcohol induced frenzy. They lay in beds with transparent white curtains closing them in, but the curtains did nothing to hide their actions.

Or to hide me from their sight, if they can see me at all around all the naked humans...

Silently, she prayed they stayed distracted until she could spot the God of Sin and get him out of there.

Her gaze moved back to the man covered in a sea of naked female flesh on the back wall. He was the only person, who wasn't an angel, having sex on one of the beds. *Is he the Immortal I'm looking for?* She moved closer to him. He was kissing a woman, even while he was buried inside another one. He lazily broke his kiss and turned to Surcy. His gaze racked her body, and he gestured for her to join him.

Immediately, she knew it was him. Something about him screamed of power and magic, but it was also something else. Unlike the angels, he didn't seem to be enjoying what he was doing. It was as if he were simply going through the motions.

Which was strange for a man lying in a bed with six naked women.

I need to touch him, or I can't teleport us out of here. She eyed the bed, not wanting to get anywhere near it, but knowing it was the only way.

Moving forward, she slid onto the only empty spot on the bed. He turned his head. His hand reached out and stroked down her back. She put her hand on his neck and tried to teleport them free.

But it didn't work.

Oh, shit. Of course there's a shield in place.

He leaned closer and nipped at her throat. "There are wards here. Once you get in, the only way out is to walk, and they'll never let us leave."

Her throat clenched. "You know who I am?"

"Yes, and I know who I am. But this place? It's my prison. A prison of sins and *delights.*"

There has to be a way. "How can we get you free?"

He bit her lower earlobe, making her skin crawl. "You can't."

His hand moved to grab her ass.

She pushed it away. "I'm not here for that."

His hand fixed more tightly onto her lower back. "And I can't stop. What was once pleasure is now torture. I'm driven by a need for sex. I can't stop. I can barely leave this bed. I've been here for what seems like lifetimes."

"We only need you to stop for a minute... just long enough to climb those stairs and run for the exit."

He groaned and the woman on top of him started rocking harder and harder. "Do you think I'd still be here if I could take those steps? No, the women they send in here take me over and over again in this bed, until they're spent, and then new ones come to replace the old."

"Pick one of them up," she suggested. "Take her with us."

"They're bound to the bed," he groaned and began to thrust. "And I can never stop. *Never*. No matter how much I want to."

He has to keep having sex. All the time. We have to get him out of this room, to the next one, where we can teleport free. Just a few dozen steps, and I've rescued this Immortal, without any bloodshed.

She counted the angels in the room. There were eight of them, too many for her to handle. *Too many.*

So, how could she get him free?

And then, it hit her. *I can't.*

But do I have a choice?

She swallowed down the bile rising in the back of her throat. "I can help you leave."

"How?" His voice was filled with desperation.

"What if we left... while having sex?"

Her words were met with silence. "I've always needed

more than one woman in this place. My incubus needs would drain a single human woman."

"But what about an angel?" she said.

His entire body shuddered behind her. "And do you often give into the pleasures of the body?"

"Only with the men I love."

"So pure," he murmured into her ear.

She wanted to scream, to leap from the bed. Hadn't they given enough to this cause? Would she really have to give this too?

You already betrayed your demons' trust. She pushed the thought aside. Frink had to be lying. She would never let Caine pick her brain. She would never betray her demons. *But I know I did.*

Anger rose inside of her. Now she did have a choice. Leave and come back with her demons. See more bloodshed. Put their lives, and the other Immortal's lives, at risk too.

Or let a incubus have sex with her.

Let someone other than her demons touch her.

Could they ever forgive me for this? She pushed the thought aside. If it kept them safe, she would do this. She would do anything for them.

"Would it work?" she pressed.

The incubus slowly turned her around, and then she was staring into his face. He had dark eyes and dark hair. He was handsome in a bad-boy kind of way. His face looked like it was constantly stuck in a state of mockery. His body was finely tuned, and his flesh was pale, like he hadn't seen sunlight for a long time.

All of it gave the look of an ancient being, capable of powerful things.

"Do you want me inside of you, angel?"

She met his gaze. "No. But we are gathering all the Immortals together for a stand against Caine. We need you. Or we'll fail."

Something troubled flashed in his eyes. "How many of the others do you have?"

"By now?" she nibbled her lip. "We should have all of them."

His brows rose. "I've never touched a woman who didn't want me. But this must be done."

Her stomach churned.

"Take off your clothes," he said, his voice soft and seductive.

She felt his incubus powers wash over her. But still, her hands trembled as she pulled off her shirt. He unbuttoned her pants, and within moments, she was lying beside him naked.

Tears filled her eyes.

He pushed the other women away. They didn't seem to notice. They simply carried on without him.

His lips slanted over Surcy's, and she felt his power like something all-consuming. Her thoughts swam. His kiss was like a drug that sent her head spinning.

She felt him pull her on top of him, straddling his waist.

And tears slid down her cheeks.

He grabbed her ass, moved his hands to her thighs, and lifted her from the bed.

She felt him, hard and aroused beneath her. More tears ran down her cheeks. She thought of her demons, of Mark's sweet face, of Tristan, of Daniel. They would never forgive her for this.

His kiss deepened, his tongue sweeping inside her mouth. His power seemed to pull from her, and with each second that passed, she felt more relaxed. Her thoughts swam as every inch of his naked flesh touched hers.

He carried them from the room. She felt them moving up the stairs.

His muscles were tense beneath her hands. She waited for him to plunge inside of her. To use her to get free of his prison.

But as she sagged against him, she realized she might not even notice. His touch drained her so powerfully.

"Teleport us," he whispered into her ear.

She fought to make sense of his words.

"Now! Get us out of here!"

She heard shouts. Feet running.

Closing her eyes, and gritting her teeth, she willed them to teleport away.

And then, everything went black.

11

S urcy startled awake. Tears were running down her face. She'd been caught in a nightmare. One in which an Immortal was fucking her over and over again, draining her of her strength.

And now? She was naked. In a hotel room. A white sheet over her body.

The God of Sin looked up from a table spread with more food than she'd ever imagined. The massive flat screen TV played a show she didn't recognize.

He grinned, showing his dimples. "You're awake."

Her entire body felt tense. "We had sex. Oh god. Oh shit."

To her surprise, his smile fell away. "We didn't. It was hard as fuck, but I've never had sex with a woman who didn't want me, and I never plan to."

"Then, how did we escape?"

"I kissed you. I forced a lot of your energy out of you, in a way that wasn't pleasant for either of us, not nearly as pleasant as just fucking. But," he shrugged, "you were crying. You clearly love the men you have."

She pressed her knuckles to her forehead and felt tears rolling down her cheeks. Nothing had happened between them. Not really. She hadn't betrayed her demons, and she'd saved the Immortal.

It was almost too much to believe.

"You barely managed to teleport us onto the street before you passed out, but it was enough. I ran us down the street, naked as hell, to the nicest hotel I could find. I seduced a human, got us this room, and showered. Oh man, you can't imagine how good that felt." Then, he held up a steak. Literally, an entire steak speared by his fork and took a huge bite. "And real food? Fucking hell, it's amazing. Not the shit they fed me in that sex dungeon."

It was strange. This Immortal was cocky, inhumanely handsome, and a incubus. She knew she should dislike a creature like him, she really should, but she just couldn't.

He'd been a slave to Caine just like all the others. *Just like me.*

She wiped her cheeks and drew her knees to her chest. "How long was I asleep?"

He stared. "All night... about eight hours, give or take."

"Damn it."

He raised a brow, studying her.

"We have to go. My demons need me. The Immortals need me. We have to find them all, make sure they're safe, and get to the sanctuary."

He frowned and took another massive bite of his steak. "So," he said while chewing. "When we find them, then we start a war?"

She nodded.

He chewed for a long minute, then swallowed. "Okay then. I ordered us some clothes. How about we enjoy this food until they get here?"

For a minute she almost said no. Her demons needed her. They must have thought she'd completely abandoned them. *Which I kind of did.* What if they were in trouble? What if they needed her?

But then, her stomach growled so loudly that the incubus raised a brow.

She sighed, wrapped the sheet around her body, and sat down on the other chair at the table. *I won't be any use to anyone starving... and naked.*

"Dig in," he said with a smile. "I'm watching this weird human show where I think the woman chooses between the men she wants. I'm assuming the losers are killed?"

Surcy laughed at his assumption. "No, human games aren't nearly as bloody now."

He looked disappointed. "Oh well, at least the clothes are skimpier."

She ate across from him, watching his excitement at the show, even at the commercials. Caine never ceased to amaze her with his evil. How could he even think to create a room in which the God of Sin, a incubus, could never stop having sex? It was like creating his own personal hell.

The Immortal finished his steak and reached for the lobster with his bare hands. "You never told me your name."

"Surcy," she answered, watching him pull out the lobster meat with enthusiasm.

"Surcy," he repeated. "Surcy the fallen angel."

"I'm not fallen," she told him.

He smiled. "Not when the Immortals come back into power. No, then you'll just be an angel again. Restored to your former glory." His gaze moved to her shoulders. "And you'll get those back too."

The scars on her shoulder blades prickled. *Is that really what would happen?* She'd never thought about her own place in the world if they won this war, just how it'd change everything for the better.

"I know who you are, but I don't know your name either."

He smiled again, butter smeared on his lips. "Zagan."

"Zagan?" Her gaze ran over the muscled man.

"It's a family name," he said, with a grin.

She watched him for a while longer while eating the most delicious mashed potatoes, a chocolate cake, and bacon bruschetta. When her stomach finally said *enough*, she leaned back in her chair and stretched.

His gaze snapped back to her, and the hunger in his eyes shocked her.

"I imagine after all you've been through, you never want to have sex again." Her words came out nervous and rushed.

His eyes darkened. "I'm the God of Sin and a incubus. Without sex, I'd wither away to nothing. But next time, it'll be by *my* choice. Maybe even with a woman who sees me as more than just a big dick. Maybe one who sees me the way you see your demons."

She was shocked by the anger and passion in his eyes. This Immortal might act cool and casual, but he was simmering with rage under his calm exterior.

A knock sounded at the door.

Zagan rose, and for the first time, she saw that he was naked. His massive cock hard and erect as he went to open the hotel room door. A minute later, a woman giggled.

A pretty blonde and the god entered the room a second later, her carrying two garment bags. He immediately took them from her and slung them on his chair.

His gaze moved to Surcy. "I think this pretty little lady might suck me off. Want to join us? Or would you prefer a shower?"

Swallowing hard, she rose from her seat, clinging to the sheet. "I think I'll take a shower."

He sat on the edge of the bed, and the woman immediately knelt before him. Her smaller hands curled around his shaft, and then she took him deep. For a second, Surcy couldn't look away. She watched them, him digging his hand into the back of her hair, her moaning around him.

I miss my demons.

The realization hit her like a brick. She scuttled away and took a long, cold shower. When she got back home, she'd find time to make love to her men again. She'd steal a tiny moment of pleasure before the war truly began.

12

Surcy stood beside the God of Sin, staring at the remains of the Immortal's house. It was burnt to the ground, leaving even the earth blackened. But mixed into it all was a shimmering blue substance she'd never seen before.

Walking forward, crunching on the burnt wood and ash, she reached down and touched it, pulling her fingers back to stare at the shimmering substance. Something wasn't adding up in her mind. What had happened here?

Are my demons okay? Her heart raced. She'd thought saving this Immortal would be easier than the God of Sin. Mark's description had made it sound so anyway. *So why is this home destroyed?*

"Fuck, I didn't know Caine had made any archangels. I thought he'd simply destroyed the ones loyal to us."

Surcy whirled on him. "What's an archangel?"

"Something you don't want to meet."

Zagan walked around the charred remains of the house and stopped near the back. Lifting his hand, palm down, he closed his eyes. Something inside of her warmed, like she was standing too close to a crackling fire. But for some reason, she just drew closer to the Immortal, like a moth to a flame.

His eyes opened, and for one moment his irises were red.

She stiffened, and the color faded away.

He blinked several times, and his jaw tensed. "Surcy, I need you to stay calm."

"Calm?"

"Yes, calm. An archangel was here. The most powerful creature an Immortal can make. They have far more freewill than normal angels. White-winged angels are like trusted soldiers. Dark-winged angels are like warriors who haven't quite proved themselves. But archangels? They have powers beyond your imagination." He took a deep breath and moved closer to her. "You know the blue flames on your sword are angel-fire, something specifically created to defeat demons. It's hotter and more destructive than normal fire, even though angels are immune to it."

Her heart was racing. "What are you trying to tell me?"

"Archangels have the power to control this fire at will. And this place—it was burnt down by angel magic."

"We need to hurry," she rushed out. "Daniel and Tristan must have faced this being. We need to find them and help them, before it can hurt them."

He grimaced. "I'm afraid we're too late."

"No."

He looked down at the charred remains of the house. "Two souls were lost in this house. A gargoyle, and a fire-mage, two beings that I feel were strongly connected to you."

Her head spun, and she crumpled to her knees.

His hands were gripping her arms in an instant. "I'm

sorry, Surcy. I am. But the Immortals didn't die here. I can sense where they've gone. We need to find them, before the archangel can."

"They're dead," she whispered.

A second later, she was swept up into his strong arms. "I'm going to start walking. We're going to find the others of my kind. You have a short time to process this, and then you need to pull it together. Your lover's souls will be before Caine soon. If you have any chance of saving them, you have to push away the pain and keep going."

She looked up at the evening sky. In this part of the world, night would be falling soon. The clouds here were heavy, dashed with the slightest bit of grey. It was just another place in the world that meant nothing to her, not without her demons.

Squeezing her eyes shut, she imagined Mark, Tristan, and Daniel. They'd all died. They died for this cause. She had to fight past the gnawing feeling in her belly that told her everything she cared about was gone. She had to push back the thoughts that were screaming that this was her fault. It'd been a risk to go after an Immortal alone and leave them to handle this one, but she'd thought she was the only one taking a risk.

Now she knew she'd been wrong.

"If you'd have been there, you'd have died too," the incubus said, as if reading her thoughts.

"I—" the word came, choked out. "Maybe. Maybe not."

"Everything happens for a reason, Surcy. We're all just pawns in Fate's games."

Her hand clenched in the front of his silk shirt. "So, you're saying we have no choice?"

He shook his head, hurrying quickly down the sidewalk. "The Fates see the future. Even they try to stop it sometimes. There are things we can do, but I can tell you with absolute certainty that your demons would have died today... in any future that might lead to the Immortals reuniting."

A tear ran down her cheek, clinging to her chin. "I never wanted this for them."

His dark eyes locked onto hers. "And we never wanted this for you, but you and your demons were always meant to suffer in this war, to pay a hefty price."

"How do you—?"

"Quiet," he hissed, sliding into an alley.

She felt his heart racing under her hand. "What is it?"

"Angels... everywhere."

He leaned slightly forward, and they both stared. Sure enough, angels walked among the humans, an angel for every two humans. There were so many that Surcy could only stare. She had no idea there were even this many in the army.

"This is bad," she whispered.

He shook his head and grinned. "No, this is good. It means they haven't found the Immortals yet."

That's true. "Any idea where they would have gone?"

He glanced down at her. "I think you can answer that question better than I can."

"No—" she froze. "Maybe."

In an instant, she teleported them.

"Fuck," Zagan muttered, collapsing onto his knees.

She slid from his grip on the roof of the building she'd first teleported the farmer and her demons onto. If the Immortals were alone, she'd think this is where they'd go.

In the skies, she spotted the dark shapes that meant angels flew overhead. "We need to be careful," she whispered.

Zagan rubbed his head and stood. "Fucking warn me next time you're going to do that."

Then, she started walking around the roof. They weren't anywhere easily spotted, but if they saw the angels, they wouldn't be. She moved to where the massive air conditioning units and vents cluttered one end of the roof. Zagan followed closely behind. Everywhere she looked was empty. And then, she spotted the little metal closet. The spot beside the lock had been kicked in.

Taking a deep breath, she inched toward it, grabbed the edge of the door, and pulled it open. The farmer was clutching a woman in his arms, stuffed in front of a space filled with wires and buttons. He held a metal pole out in front of him, ready to swing.

His eyes widened when he spotted her and he dropped the pole. "Thank God, it's you."

She could sense the angels flying closer, to the point that it was hard to breathe. There were now three Immortals and only one of her, and enemies everywhere. She had no chance of protecting these people in her care.

Zagan leaned in. "Hey guys, how's this life treating you? I know that last one sucked, and the one before that, and, " he laughed, "well, you get the picture."

We don't have time for this. Not if we want to live.

Surcy didn't wait for their answers. She grabbed onto them and teleported away.

They hit the ground outside of the sanctuary.

"Fucking hell!" Zagan shouted. "Didn't I just say not to do that? Angels always love that shit, and it's annoying. It gives me a damn headache."

She laughed, even though the sound was painful. "We just escaped an army of angels. Let's be glad. And let's hurry and reach the others. We have a war to fight."

Zagan shot her a dirty glance, but reached a hand down to help the woman up.

Her cheeks turned red. "I'm Nichole."

He raised a brow. "No, you're the Goddess of Life, and you and I have always had a lot of fun together."

She visibly swallowed. "Have we?"

He flashed her his dimples. "And we'll have fun in this life too."

The farmer climbed to his feet, and Surcy led them through the barrier to the lands surrounding the sanctuary. A shiver ran down her spine as the power made goose bumps rise on her arms. The shield around this place had been reinforced by the druids since she left.

Good.

"Are my wife and kids here?" Clarence asked at her side.

Oh no. She took a deep breath. "Your kids are. And they're safe."

"And my wife?" There was a little more intensity to the question.

"She—she was stabbed by one of the angels. I dropped her off at a hospital."

His voice shook. "Is she okay?"

Heart in her throat, she raised her eyes to meet his. "I don't know. I had to leave before I could find out."

"You need to go see," he said.

She shook her head. "We can't. There's a war to fight."

"I don't care!"

Zagan and the woman froze beside them.

"Something wrong?" Zagan asked.

"My wife's hurt, and she's saying we can't go and check on her."

Zagan shrugged. "A marriage between an Immortal and a human is always short. It's better to focus on protecting the afterlife of all of humanity rather than one woman."

Clarence glared at the man. "Would you say that if she were your wife?"

Tension sung between them.

Zagan's gaze slid between them. "Let's get to the sanctuary and then we'll decide what to do."

They started walking again. After a moment, Clarence followed, looking angry. The woman dropped back to keep pace with him, and Surcy tried to tune out her whispers.

"We'll get them in the water," Zagan said. "They'll get back their memories, and their powers, and he'll remember what's important."

"I hope so," Surcy said, but deep in her heart she wasn't sure.

Love was a powerful thing. And this war? She might just give it all up to be back with her demons.

Unfortunately for her, she didn't have that choice.

They continued trekking through the woods, but in her mind, she was far away, in the arms of three demons who made her smile. Who made her feel safe.

And who she might have lost forever.

13

The sanctuary was complete chaos, filled with people talking, laughing, and moving about. Surcy watched as the Immortals they had rescued earlier dunked the new ones into the pool to awaken their memories and their powers.

The God of Sin fucked a druid woman in one corner. None of them could see what was happening, but all of them could hear her shouts of pleasure.

Zagan had winked at Surcy beforehand. "I think she deserves a little happiness after serving us so faithfully," he said as he led her over behind a tree.

Now, it sounded like he was determined to give it to her. Hard and long.

Which is pretty damn awkward...

The other Immortals seemed to all be doing their own thing, a few practicing their magic. Others ate and relaxed. And some of them needed healing and they were being tended to by the druids, who all seemed happy in their service.

And Surcy? She was sitting on a pedestal carved of stone, staring at it all numbly.

She and her demons had talked about this moment for so long. This was their goal, the thing they imagined might be impossible. Now, they'd actually accomplished it. All the Immortals were safe. They had the ability to destroy Caine and restore the balance of the realms.

But her demons weren't at her side.

Of all the futures she imagined, this was not one of them. Losing her demons hadn't felt possible.

The God of Summer, a shifter who could turn into a golden dragon, met her gaze. He moved confidently across the great sanctuary, that was enclosed by a massive dome covered in plants. He wore a simple white shirt and jeans. His skin and hair were both golden, and his eyes were immensely powerful.

Kneeling down in front of her, he cocked his head, and studied her. She was amazed by how strong he appeared, how muscular and healthy. It was almost unimaginable that just a short time ago he was a chained dragon, with grey, lifeless scales and holes in his wings.

They'd saved him. She'd imagined he was powerful beneath all his wounds. But now, she could see what he was meant to be, and it amazed her.

"You're heartbroken," he said, his voice deep and rough.

It was hard to swallow. "Yes."

"Then let me ease your fears. If we are restored to power, we should be able to save your demons."

Every muscle in her body tensed. "What if Caine destroys their souls?"

A guarded look came over his face. "The Soul Destroyer is not what everyone believes."

She waited.

"It is simply... another realm."

She slid closer to him, heart racing. "So, they can be saved?"

"If they survive. The Soul Destroyer was not given that name lightly. Within that realm is the darkest, most horrible place in existence. It is filled with souls deemed too dangerous to be reborn. They don't have to survive just going there. They need to survive within the realm."

Her chest swelled. "They're strong. They can do that."

The slightest smile twisted his lips. "They are. Your demons are unlike any I've met before. But then, I've never known demons to fall in love with an angel, or an angel to fall in love with them. Caine... he's created a world of chaos. One which we must fix."

"Surcy?"

She startled, looking up to meet Mark's father's eyes.

"Yes?"

"May I speak with you for just a moment?"

She nodded, then turned back to the dragon-shifter. "Thank you."

"Any of us would have shared that knowledge with you."

She smiled. That didn't matter. He was the one who had taken the time to tell her. "Not for the knowledge, for the hope."

He shrugged. "I was hopeless when you and your demons found me. It seems only fair to give you hope in return."

She smiled and rose. Mark's father turned and started walking. She followed slowly behind him. When they came to the mantel before the Immortals' sacred pool, he reached up and took the broken staff from off of it.

Her breath hitched. *Mark's staff.*

"I know what you must think of me. Throwing my only child out into the world alone and without his staff."

"Well, whatever you did didn't break him. Nothing could break him."

The old man turned his blue eyes to her and her heart clenched again. Mark and his father had the same eyes. "He is... was something special."

"You have no idea how much." Surcy didn't even try to hold back the anger that surged through her.

No matter how she replayed what had led Mark to be tossed from his home, she couldn't see any justification for it. No matter how hard she tried to see this old man in a different light, she only felt anger towards him for the cruel way he'd treated her Mark.

"I still can't believe he's dead."

She felt her gut clench. "I'm done talking to you about this."

You don't deserve to feel sad, or to pity yourself. You closed the door on your child a long time ago.

He sighed. "I actually wanted to talk to you about more than just Mark."

The sensation of fingers moving down her spine made every hair on her body stand on end. "Then what? Spit it out."

The old man set the staff back down and turned to her. "I've been reading over the ancient texts, including what little we have about the time when Caine took over and the Immortals lost their thrones."

She held her breath.

"Something is missing."

No shit, if we knew everything this whole mess wouldn't be nearly as bad.

"Have you ever heard about demi-gods?"

She raised a brow. "Like half-gods?"

"Yes, the children of the Immortals."

She shook her head.

"Well, they're rare, and most of them have little to no power. Their power might be something as small as being particularly lucky, or living abnormally long, or being incredible beautiful. Something small like that couldn't unbalance the Immortals' power. But—" he paused. "Then, there is Caine. He's not a vampire, a witch, a merman, a gargoyle... nothing about him makes sense. He lacks the characteristics of any of the paranormal beings."

"So what does that mean?"

He held her gaze. "I believe he might be something... forbidden, a dark secret that should have never been brought to life."

That sounds... bad.

Her heart raced. "What?"

"A child of two Immortals."

She stared. "I don't understand. I mean, why would that be so forbidden?"

He regarded her as if she were stupid. "Because there has only ever been ten Immortals. For this very reason. It's too dangerous. It can change the balance. And yet..."

"What?"

"The balance doesn't feel off."

She sighed, tired of the old man's riddles. "And what does that mean?"

"I believe there is a twelfth Immortal."

Her brows rose. "So we need to find one more?"

"No, you don't. But what you should know is that Caine is even more dangerous than we ever imagined, and these Immortals may have secrets that could complicate our plans."

Like we need more complications. "Thank you."

He nodded. "I wish we druids could offer you our help in the battle, but that is not our way."

Mark did. "I understand."

Turning away, she wondered what the significance of twelve Immortals might mean, and how it could impact the war between the two sides. *I guess we'll see.*

urcy lay on the grass, staring up at the bright moon. She'd left the warmth and comfort of the inner-sanctuary, where all the Immortals and druids lay sleeping amongst the magic plants, to take a quiet moment to herself. Tomorrow, they would attack Zudessa. They would take on Caine and his angels. Either the battle would destroy them all, along with all hope at a better world, or everything would change forever.

For some reason, both futures scared her.

This was everything that they'd been working toward, but now the unknown loomed in front of her, and for once, she felt empty when she imagined the future. Tristan had said he'd bought them three days before Mark's soul was destroyed, but did he and Daniel have the same time?

Or had she already lost them?

And can the Immortals really bring them back if that's where they were sent? For some reason, she couldn't imagine it could be that simple. She didn't want to think about what her demons might be facing in such a terrible place.

It's possible they can't survive there.

The moon blurred in her vision as her eyes filled with tears. She didn't know the answers, but an emptiness clawed at her center, one she feared meant her demons were lost to her forever.

"Surcy?"

She shot up, and her gaze connected with Clarence's. No, not Clarence, the God of the Earth. After dipping into the waters, he'd announced that he hated his human-name for this lifetime, and that everyone could call him Adan.

"Do you need something?" she asked, frowning.

He glanced down at something in his hand, a little vial that seemed to contain nothing but water. His expression was uncertain as he shifted it between his fingers.

"Yes, angel. I know that you don't work for us... but I have need of you."

His words vibrated through her in the strangest way. She touched her chest and frowned.

"You felt it didn't you?" he asked.

"What was that?" she whispered.

"That, is how it feels when your ruler speaks to you. Once we're in charge once more, that feeling will grow stronger when we give a command. When we wish something, you'll all feel it deep within you. It isn't in the forceful way that Caine commands you. It will be something more natural. Because that's the way it was meant to be." He moved a little closer, his gaze holding hers. "We trusted Caine. We never imagined he would be capable of what he did. But as much as he thinks he seamlessly rules in our place, he doesn't. If anyone remembered what it was like before, they'd know how much was missing."

She believed him, but that wasn't what bothered her. "So, when all this is over, I'll serve you?"

He nodded, lifting a brow. "Isn't that what you desire most? Isn't that why you've done all of this for?"

I did it because the world was wrong, because innocent people were suffering in the demon realm, and angels were mostly heartless thugs.

And because my demons convinced me to help them.

Not so I could serve a better leader.

Slowly, she shook her head. "No. I mean, I never thought about what things would be like for me if we restored the ten of you to power."

He didn't speak, just waited, watching her closely.

"After you're back on your thrones, will I be able to be with my demons?"

"We'll judge souls fairly and place them where they should have been all along. Things will be very different, Surcy. Definitely more fair. But I can't guarantee where you and your loved ones will end up."

After all we've done! After all my demons sacrificed to help these people, they really won't even give us this? Anger blossomed inside her, but she forced it down. Anger would get her nowhere.

And when her anger faded away, it was replaced with nothing but a painful emptiness in her chest.

"I understand," she said.

Then both looked at the moon for a long minute, a sadness that seemed soul-deep stretching between them. She wanted to beg him for special treatment. She wanted to tell him, after all they'd done, they should be exempt from judgment. But she couldn't.

"Love is complicated," he said. "It goes against all reason. Believe me. Love led me to one of the greatest mistakes I could make. And yet, I don't regret it."

Tears pricked her eyes as she imagined the faces of her

demons. Goose bumps rose on her flesh, as if they even her skin missed the touch of the men she loved.

"I need you to go to my human-wife and make her drink this."

She looked at him and then down at the water he held. "Why?"

"It's from the pool. Going in the water is deadly for any but Immortals, but there's a legend about the water's ability to heal. If she doesn't seem to be recovering on her own, I want you to make her drink it." He held out the vial, but she didn't take it.

"Are you sure?"

He sighed, noisily. "I know I should be above things like this. I know I shouldn't care for one human female, but that's why love is such a weakness. It defies all logic."

Reaching out, she plucked the vial from his fingers. It wasn't that she was looking forward to a long night when she'd be battling in the morning; it was that she felt she owed this man. It was her fault his wife was injured. Maybe if the woman lived, she would provide an anchor for him, to help him remember that humans had value.

So he could never end up like Caine.

Rising, she started walking, knowing that it would take a while to reach the edge of the sanctuary. But, his voice stopped her. "Just in case we can't save your demons' souls, it might be a good idea to mourn them tonight, so their deaths can't be used against you."

She felt every muscle in her body tense. *Are these Immortals trying to drive me insane? Can they be saved or not?* It felt... terrible not to know.

Without answering him, she kept moving, but tears ran down her cheeks. Maybe a plan like that would work for him. For her, if she didn't have hope, she wouldn't be able to keep going.

So, she'd hold onto the belief that her demons could be saved, regardless of the odds against her.

The forest was quiet. With each step she took further from the sanctuary, she prayed for clarity. She prayed she would know what to do when the time came. When she finally felt the prickling as she crossed the protective barrier, she inhaled deeply. She prepared herself for the hospital, and for the truth of what happened to the human woman.

The hairs on the back of her neck prickled.

Turning, she stared into the darkness. There was a terrible feeling deep in her soul, a sense that she was being hunted by a bloodthirsty predator. Every instinct begged her to retreat to the sanctuary, but she was rooted in place.

In the shadows between trees, she saw two eyes staring at her. Dark eyes held death, but also something familiar. The creature moved closer into the light.

Daniel! She gasped when she recognized the crouching form. Daniel's face was as familiar to her as her own. She knew his dark eyes, his blond hair, and his chiseled good looks that hid the vulnerable man inside. This time, however, his expression sent her blood racing.

"Daniel?" she whispered, inching closer. "Is that you?"

He rose from his crouched position, still mostly in shadows.

She longed to touch him, and the urge to throw herself into his arms was a need that burned through her.

"I thought you'd died. I thought I'd lost you." Her fingers grew sweaty around the vial clenched between them.

And then, his voice came, familiar and yet strange. "I did die. And I was reborn."

She froze, heart in her throat.

He stepped forward, his dark angel wings spread behind him. "And now, traitor, I'm here to end your life."

15

Surcy couldn't breathe, couldn't think. Daniel was an angel? That was impossible. Why would Caine do such a thing? It was dangerous! Stupid!

Before she could even process what had happened, Daniel leapt at her.

They crashed into the forest floor, and he spun on top of her. She tried to fight against him, but he was too strong, and she was confused, unwilling to hurt him.

He pinned her hands above her head with no effort at all. He looked down at her, his faces inches from hers. "Any last words?"

"I love you," she whispered.

His brows drew together in confusion. "What? You... you seem familiar."

"He erased your memories." Somewhere in the back her mind she'd known it, but it finally came together. "He erased your memories and sent you to kill the woman you love."

He frowned. "No, Caine sent me to kill a traitor. I could never love someone who rebelled against our Judge."

She laughed and looked to the heavens. "This has to be some kind of joke, or it's a terrible irony."

He settled more solidly on top of her. "What do you mean?"

Her gaze met his, and she laughed again. "Caine is an asshole. I was an angel, and you guys convinced me to love you. You convinced me to abandon everything for you and your cause. Then, the asshole captures me and erases my memories. When that doesn't work, he turns you into an angel and erases your memories too. It's like a giant joke he's playing, and I just kind of figure the only thing I can do at this point is laugh about it."

"I don't believe any of your bullshit," he said, glaring.

She made a shrugging motion, even if her shoulders didn't have anywhere to move with him holding her down. "If you don't think you love me, kiss me."

His eyes widened.

Where the hell did that idea come from? Maybe it was because of all the fairy tales about a true love's kiss breaking a spell. Or maybe it was because if she going to die, she wanted one last kiss. Either way, it was all she could think about now.

He regarded her curiously. "So, this story of yours... if I kiss you, and feel nothing, then I'll know you're a liar."

"I guess." She licked her lips. "Unless you're scared to."

He smirked, his expression so familiar it twisted her heart. "All right."

Without releasing her wrists, he shifted, sliding lower. He was so much larger, he surrounded every inch of her with his huge body. Everything inside of her warmed, aching for his kiss, aching for his closeness.

His mouth moved closer. His head tilted, and he caught her lips.

For one powerful moment, time stood still. Fire blazed between them, and the kiss grew deeper and deeper. His mouth softened over hers as their tongues tangled in the age-old dance.

She moaned and arched against him.

His cock hardened and he settled lower over her, grinding between her thighs.

Her head spun. She tried to get her hands free, to touch him, but his grip only tightened.

In her mind, she wanted this to be like the times he was rough with her. Where he did exactly what he wanted with her body—exactly what she wanted him to do.

Unfortunately, his grip was not that of a lover. This angel might be enjoying her kiss, but he still planned to kill her.

The realization crawled in the back of her mind like a serpent, curling around her thoughts, and spoiling their kiss. He moved her wrists so they were held by only one of his hands.

She tensed, knowing what was to come.

Tossing her head, she broke their kiss. He clenched a flaming sword over her head, ready to take her life.

He was breathing hard. "That was... nice. But it changes nothing."

She nodded.

The sword came down, and she jerked her body with all her might.

Her hands broke free. His sword plunged into the earth, where her throat had been just seconds before. She rolled him, so that he was beneath her, and called her own soul-blade forth. Instantly, it was in her free-hand, near his throat.

"Do it," he hissed.

She stared down at him. Could she really kill him?

No. I can't.

So what could she do?

Her hand squeezed around the little vial in her hand, and she froze. The Immortal had said it could heal. Could it heal Daniel? And could she really use it for the man she loved instead of his wife?

I can always get more.

It was a struggle to pull the cork with one hand, but she never took her gaze from his. She had no idea what this water would do. If it didn't work, she had no idea what her next step would be.

She couldn't kill Daniel, but she couldn't let him kill her.

When the cork popped free, she took a deep breath, and moved it to his lips. "Drink."

He frowned as she poured the water into his mouth, and then, he spit it out. The liquid dripped over his face, and over her.

"You idiot!" she said. "You fucking idiot!"

That was her only plan to bring him back, to restore his memories, and he'd just destroyed their only chance.

"Kill me!" he growled.

She sent her soul-blade away. "No, I love you."

In an instant, she was tossed back. She turned, trying to crawl away from him. She just needed enough space to clear her thoughts enough to teleport, but he was on her in an instant, pinning her to the ground.

It was hard to breathe beneath him. He pinned her arms above her head, yet again, and his weight kept her belly firmly on the ground.

"What now?" she asked.

He said nothing. She felt him shivering and jerking behind her. But he had her pinned so heavily that she couldn't even turn to see what he planned.

And then, he moved both of her wrists into one of his hands once again. She knew this time he wouldn't fail. He'd kill her, and there was nothing she could do to stop it.

Closing her eyes, she was surprised when she felt his hand move onto her hip and slide between her belly and the ground. He shifted slightly so that he wasn't pinning her as flatly, and then his hand dipped into the front of her pants.

Every muscle in her body tensed. "Daniel."

"Oh fuck, Surcy," he whispered. "I died. I thought I lost you."

She was breathing hard. His hand moved into her underwear, and his fingers slid into her folds, stroking her slowly. "You—remember."

"Everything," he groaned. "And now, I need to bury myself inside of you."

To feel close again. To forget everything but this moment.

"Yes," she moaned, grinding against his hand.

The silence of the woods seemed to wrap around them, to protect them from the world, if only for a short time.

His thumb brushed her clit, and she gasped. He continued to slide slowly inside her, deepening her arousal, making her ready for him. And it felt...unreal, yet perfect. Exactly what she needed. Not just sex, but to connect with him again.

Her nerves cried out in pleasure as he touched her faster. And then, one of his fingers slid deep into her channel.

She couldn't breathe. Oh god, she couldn't think. She'd never wanted anyone inside her more than she wanted him that moment.

It made it so easy to forget. So easy to live for just that moment.

And then, he slid his hand out of her pants.

"No," she murmured. "Daniel, I want—"

"I know," he said, biting her shoulder blade gently.

He fumbled with the button and zipper on her pants, then drew her pants and underwear down. A second later, she heard him taking off his own pants. She tried to move, but his hand still held her wrists down. It was strangely... erotic. Being taken in the forest like this, being fucked on grass and leaves.

Suddenly, his hard erection was sliding along her folds from behind.

She felt the shudder move through his body.

"You're so beautiful," he whispered. "So wet and ready."

She opened her mouth to speak, to say what she didn't know, but he plunged deeply inside her. A strangled sound escaped her lips, and then he was fucking her like a wild animal. The sounds of their flesh slapping against each other filled the silence. His cock was massive, almost too big, from behind, but it also felt so good her body was screaming for it to never stop.

It was all so overwhelming. So hot. The way he pinned her hands down. The way he slammed into her with such abandon, swearing softly through gritted teeth as he plunged in and out.

When a shudder moved through her body, and her inner-muscles tightened around him, his grip on her hip tightened too. "You coming, sweet Surcy?"

"Yes," she moaned.

"Then come," he ordered her, and his shaft swelled within her.

Her orgasm came, like a wave. She wished she had something to hold on to as she crashed over the edge, screaming his name. He rocked inside of her, his seed exploding and a guttural roar squeezing from his lips.

When she at last felt her muscles relax, and her body and mind connected once more, she lay panting on the ground, not moving. He lay quietly on top of her, only for a minute, before he pulled his cock free.

Without releasing her wrists, he wedged his tip into her from behind.

She tensed. "You ready for my ass?"

He slid deeper, even as her muscles squeezed around him in protest. "Always."

His hand moved from her hip to her slick folds. He began to work her again, causing the sensitive nerves to fire off in a sensation that bordered on painful. But with each movement he made, his shaft slid deeper and deeper into her, until he could go no further.

And then, he took her, slower than before. He stroked and touched her with each thrust until the sensation deep within her was a need to explode once more.

This time when her orgasm hit, it was deeper and louder, shuddering through her body like an earthquake. When she felt him come inside her, she was still shaking from the aftermath of her orgasm.

16

For a long minute, neither of them moved. Finally, he released her hands and they redressed. Before she could stand, he pulled her into his lap.

"Sorry. There was nothing in my mind—of you, of Tristan, or of Mark. Suddenly, someone pulled back the shades, and I could see all of it. I was scared, scared that if I let go of you for one minute, I'd forget it all."

She rested her head against his chest. "It's okay. I'm just glad to have you back."

More than glad. More than anything I can describe.

He kissed the top of her head and stroked her hair. Neither of them spoke for a long time. The sounds of the woods returned. The insects and birds. The whistling of the wind. It was like the world had begun to turn once more.

"I'm an angel," he whispered.

She tried to keep her words even. "How does it feel?"

His hand stilled in her hair. "Too natural. And yet, like I've been collared."

She nodded. "As long as Caine's in charge, he has far too much power over us."

He continued to stroke her hair. "So what do we do?"

What can we do? "Are Mark and Tristan angels too?"

Daniel stiffened. "I don't think so. I never saw them or sensed them."

Something she hadn't known was there began to ache, and she realized something terrible. When she'd seen Daniel, she'd naturally assumed they'd all been turned into angels. It was twisted and awful, but at least it meant they weren't beyond her grasp.

But what if it was only Daniel who had been spared?

"We have to accept they might be gone," he said. A shiver rocked violently through Daniel's body. "He shattered Tristan. And he burnt me alive."

"Who?" she whispered.

"The archangel. He's more powerful than any being I've faced except Caine."

"So, we'll have to be prepared for him tomorrow too."

Daniel stiffened. "Don't tell me anything. Caine can get inside my mind. He can order me back at any time."

"So what do we do?"

He was quiet for too long. "I go back. And I pretend that I don't remember anything. You do whatever you have planned. And when the time comes, I help."

Tears choked her throat. "I don't want you to leave. I don't want to send you back there, or do this alone."

He kissed her hair. "Me neither, but we have to."

The dark night slid into the slightest shade of grey. She stared at it, knowing it meant their time together was slipping away. With all their powers, neither one of them had the one they really needed. To stop time.

"I have to go, or he'll know something went wrong."

She clenched the fabric of his shirt in her hand. "What will you say?"

He laughed, the sound so familiar it spoke to her very soul. "I'll think of something. Lying isn't exactly a weakness of mine."

They rose, and he held her in a tight hug for one more painful moment. When she pulled back, he had the saddest smile. "I love you."

"I love you too," she whispered, and then he teleported away.

Heart in her throat, she stared at where he'd been for one long moment, before she too teleported away. Just inside the hospital, she watched an old man stiffen as his gaze fell upon her.

At the front desk, when Surcy asked about the Immortal's wife, no one knew. Surcy moved from one room to the next until she met an ICU doctor. He immediately knew the nameless stabbing victim, and just as quickly informed her that the woman had died.

She left feeling as if she'd swallowed a rock. The news would not be easy to tell the Immortal, or his children.

When she teleported back outside the sanctuary, she froze in shock. Where the woods had once been, the ground was leveled... leaving nothing behind but ash. For acres upon acres, stretching on for miles, nothing remained of the sacred grounds.

In shock, she took a step forward, stepping onto the ash that still smoldered. This was impossible. She'd only been gone for what? An hour? Two?

And then, she looked at the ash.

Kneeling down, she picked up the hot substance. Flakes of blue shone back at her.

The archangel.

17

"Did you really think they'd be safe here forever?"

Surcy whirled to stare at the most massive angel she'd ever seen. He had large red wings, corded arms, and a cruel face. Power hummed from him, power and something she couldn't quite place.

"Kneel," he ordered, and the word vibrated through her.

She collapsed onto her knees, even as she fought his control.

He moved closer until he stood just above her. "It's such a strange thing. I could order you to do anything. To suck my dick. To cut your own head off. And you'd do it. You'd have to do it."

Her muscles jerked as she fought his control over her. But no matter how hard she tried, her body remained under his control. Sweat slid down her forehead, and her breathing was rapid.

"Why are you doing this?"

The angel smirked. "I could pretend it was because Caine ordered me to. But it's not. I, in fact, have my own agenda that has nothing to do with Caine or those damn arrogant Immortals."

"What is it then?" she asked, almost afraid to know the answer.

He knelt down until his face was level with hers. "What do you know about the Soul Destroyer?"

"Nothing," she hissed, but it was painful to speak the lie.

"Such a pointless game." He reached forward and trailed a fingertip down her cheek.

She jerked away from his touch. "Just leave. You've gotten what you wanted. You've destroyed this place."

"Tell me what you know of the Soul Destroyer."

This time, she felt his power like a hand around her heart, and the words bubbled up. "It's just another realm, a place where the worst creatures imaginable are thrown."

A smile touched his lips. "I always suspected as much." His gaze grew distant, and he stood fully once more. "But Caine will never let me near it."

"What do you want with it anyway?"

He glanced at her, as if remembering her for the first time. "I don't have the power to rule the human realm, the angel realm, or the demon realm. But there? There I could have everything."

No wonder Caine made this asshole an archangel. He's just like him, already drunk on power.

He reached out and grasped her face painfully. "You've helped me in more ways than you can imagine, so, I'll give you this."

Suddenly, an image was pressed into her mind of a space just outside of Zudessa. There, the Immortals and druids lay in a pie of smoking bodies, covered in ash, their skin blackened by smoke.

"All of them still live," he whispered. "If I killed them,

Caine might get what he wanted, but I wouldn't. If you want any chance at winning this war, you'll have to hurry... before the angels find them."

When he released her face, she could feel the bruises from where his fingers had gripped her. Turning, he walked across the ash, his feet crunching with each step. When he reached the road, he looked back at her.

"If I make it into the Soul Destroyer, I'll say hi to your demons."

In the blink of an eye, the archangel was gone. The pressure of his command instantly lessened, and she shot to her feet, trembling. *So Caine did destroy their souls.*

Clenching her teeth together, she called her soul-blade into her hand and teleported. Instantly, the smell of blood hit her nostrils. Her eyes flashed open, and she saw the scene from her mind, only it was so much worse. The Immortals and the druids looked... dead. Like a pile of burned bodies.

Heart in her throat, she moved to them, placed a hand on the chest of someone she didn't recognize, and sure enough, felt the rise and fall of his or her breath. Looking past the barrier that surrounded Zedussa, she saw the angels gathering in the sky. They would be upon them within minutes. She had to do something! She had to get them to safety!

But did she have the power to do it?

Closing her eyes, she sent a silent prayer that she did, and gathered her magic.

Soon she would either save them all, or doom them.

18

The Goddess of Sacrifice blinked her eyes open. She'd never been in this much pain before. It was mind-numbing, and yet she could feel every broken bone, every cut leaking warm blood from her body.

Staring at a stone ceiling far above, with the small opening in which angels flew by, she knew exactly where she was, and who she faced.

"You're awake?"

Her head dropped slightly to one side. She stared at the dark cloud that swallowed the entire side of the throne room. But in the cloud of darkness, she knew Caine watched her, drinking in her suffering.

"I know what you think," he said, his voice sliding over her flesh like slime. "That you were powerful enough to stand against me and survive."

Blood leaked from her lips. "No," she said, her voice barely louder than a whisper. "I simply knew there was nothing more you could do to me that hasn't been done already."

"You're referencing your rape, beating, and death?" He

laughed. "Oh believe me, child, that's nothing in comparison to what I can do to you."

Something within her shriveled back in fear. Something she hated.

It was her damned heart. It remained human, no matter what she did. It ached when she took lives. It felt like an open, gaping wound each time her memories turned her dreams into nightmares.

Her heart was the one thing she wished to be rid of more than anything else in this world. She cared nothing for the war, for the angels and the demons, or for anything except for a way to stop the pain that made her every breath pure torture.

She'd been so close to achieving her dream.

She'd felt the gargoyle die. She'd held his stone-essence in her hand, ready to devour it. To kill the last thing that was human within her. But Caine's angels had invaded her fortress before she could, killing her guards and taking her prisoner.

Now, she cared nothing for what this power-hungry fool did to her. She only wanted the stone-essence back.

"Looking for this?" Caine's voice came, filled with humor, and a hand emerged from the darkness, holding the gargoyle's essence as it pulsed.

She tried to roll toward it and gasped. She cried out as the pain roared through her, blackening her vision. She needed that essence, needed it more than she needed air.

"I have thought long and hard over how to make you suffer for your betrayal." The cloud moved toward her, and she sensed him coming closer.

But her gaze was locked on the gargoyle's essence. If Caine got close enough, she would snatch it from him. At that point, no matter what happened to her body or soul, she wouldn't care.

The throne room doors were thrown open. Four men, surrounded by angels, were bound together. Their heads and hands were locked in thick wooden stocks that they carried on their massive backs. The men looked wild and dangerous.

They were exactly the kind of men she feared.

Trailing behind them all was an old woman, less battered than she was, but a lot filthier.

"Do it," Caine said, and his voice was like a coiled snake.

The old woman shuffled closer to her and knelt down. "I'm sorry," she whispered. "But it's the only way he'll let me go."

The Demon of Sacrifice tried to escape the woman, but her injuries made it impossible.

The old woman began to chant a spell, a witch's curse. She plunged a glowing red hand into The Demon of Sacrifice's chest. The pain... it was on another level. It went beyond her body and soul, to her very heart.

When the demon's vision cleared, she saw the woman holding a pulsing ghostly heart in her hands. And she knew, she could *feel*, that it was her own. The witch rose to her feet and moved to the four frightening prisoners.

She hesitated.

"Do it," Caine commanded, his voice shaking with rage or excitement, she wasn't sure which.

The witch tore the heart into four equal pieces while the demon screamed and withered upon the ground. When the witch was done, she forced the pieces, one after another, into the men. When she was done, the men were on their knees, panting and glaring.

"It's done," the witch said.

The demon lay upon her back, shaking in shock. She felt different. Her emotions didn't make sense, and her chest felt empty and strange. "What did you do to me?"

"Simple," Caine whispered. "You betrayed me for this fucking stone heart. And so, I have given you the perfect punishment. These four men now control your heart. They hold the pieces, connecting you to them forever."

"No," she whispered.

"It's like being in love," he said, his voice amused. "Only, you don't have a choice."

She heard him snap his fingers. The angels grabbed each man, and then they were gone.

"Wh—what?"

"Oh, did I not mention? Not only do they hold your heart, but if you want to find them, you'll have to work for it." He laughed. "Now guards, taken her broken body and toss it outside the barrier. Let's see how long it takes her to heal with birds picking at her flesh."

Two angels grabbed her. She screamed at the pain their touch brought. Her head lolled to the side between them, and she wished for death. She wished real death would come, the kind that meant her suffering would finally end.

The old witch, wearing nothing but scraps of cloth, knelt down, her body filthy and thin.

"My freedom," she whispered, her voice cracking.

"Of course," he said, annoyance in his voice. He gestured with his hands. "Guards, take her back to the dungeons."

Two angels grabbed her arms. The woman began to fight, her voice rising. "You gave me your word! You said—"

"I'm sorry, but you're far too valuable for me to let go."

As the Demon of Sacrifice was carried out of the fortress and to the desert outside, she heard the sounds of the witch's sobs. She wanted to be happy. The witch had doomed her to a life of unimaginable suffering. But her heart? The pieces of it, that she could sense even now, ached to return to her.

Her thoughts came again, swimming through her pain. If Caine thought he'd won, he was wrong. He had no idea what she was capable of. She would track down the four men, and she'd recover her heart. Then, she'd find Caine, get her stone-essence, and make him pay.

He might be powerful, but I'm The Demon of Sacrifice. Revenge against men is what I do.

19

S urcy somehow managed to teleport the entire group of people to the little cabin Daniel had brought her to so long ago. She wasn't sure if was the exertion of teleporting that many people at one time, or her exhaustion, but she immediately collapsed, falling into darkness.

When she awoke, she was lying on a bed, with the God of Earth's two children asleep beside her.

She sat up and found herself surrounded by Immortals. To her complete shock, all of them appeared to be entirely healed. Their hair had returned and their skin was no longer burnt and blackened.

It was... impossible, a miracle. And yet, as she watched, she noticed a stiffness to their movements.

So maybe they still have more healing to do.

Her body ached as she pulled back the covers and slipped from the bed.

The Goddesses of Winter and Spring glanced up at her from where they crowded near the fire.

"The angel's awake," The Goddess of Winter said.

Her words had an immediate effect on the room. All eyes turned to her, with a mixture of relief and unease.

Adan, the God of the Earth, left the kitchen and came to stand in front of her. "My wife?"

Her heart lurched, and she shook her head.

For a minute, a look of pure pain came over his face, and then it disappeared. "Humans always go too fast."

The Goddess of Winter moved closer, and Surcy felt an immediate chill. "I wish to speak with you. In private."

Surcy almost groaned. *What could this be about now?*

Wincing, she followed the goddess outside. To her shock, the God of Sin followed too. The other Immortals stared at them as they passed, and there was an unspoken tension she didn't understand.

On the porch, they sat around a little table, no one speaking for a time.

At last, the God leaned back, exhaling loudly. "We fucked up."

She raised a brow in confusion.

"Caine, the bastard. The monster who tortured all of us for so many lifetimes. The man who screwed up every fucking realm. He's our son."

Her brain stopped. She looked between the two of them.

The Goddess of Winter stared out at the sky, her gaze troubled. "It was one night of pleasure. We convinced ourselves when I got pregnant that he couldn't possibly be the father." She gestured to the God of Sin as she spoke. "We'd had many other partners, and the coupling of Gods had never before resulted in a pregnancy."

"But we were wrong," he said. "We didn't know it until it was too late. We kept him in the fortress. We watched him carefully. He showed more power than our demi-god children, but not much. We didn't know until he attacked what he was capable of."

Okay... that was unexpected.

"Why are you telling me all of this? I know he's your son, but you know we still have to kill him, right?"

He laughed. "Of course you have to kill him. He's a monstrous mistake that we both regret terribly."

The Goddess of Winter spoke, her voice barely louder than a whisper. "I thought if I was kind to him. If I was patient with him. That even if he was... our child, he wouldn't be the wretched creature that the Fates warned about." She wrapped her arms around herself. "But there was always evil within him, I just didn't see it."

He sneered. "It wasn't entirely our fault. It was about the balance. If she hadn't have been so pure and good—"

"There is no one to blame for this but us," the goddess interrupted, her words like a slap.

Tension sliced between the two Immortals. Zagan looked as he really wanted to say more, but he kept his mouth shut.

"I'm sorry," Surcy said, not knowing what else to say.

The Goddess seemed not to hear her. "We just wanted you to know that he's more dangerous than you ever imagined. When the time comes, we have to kill him without hesitation."

Surcy opened her mouth to offer some reassurance.

"Go," the goddess whispered, but it wasn't a command, more like a plea.

Surcy turned back to the door, but looked at them one last time. The God of Sin had moved to stand behind her, even though they didn't touch. A single tear slid down the goddess's face, but froze midway on her cheek.

What must it be like to know your child is evil? And to know he'll be killed? Her heart twisted, and she slipped back inside.

The cabin was strangely quiet, as if the Immortals were lying about preparing for war in some unseen way. She went to the kitchen, ate and drank, then showered.

When she finished her shower, the Goddess of Winter and the God of Sin had returned to the room, each on different sides. All eyes turned to Surcy.

Uh oh.

"So what now?" The God of Night, a vampire with a hell of an attitude, asked. Something in his dark expression told her he was angry.

Surcy decided to just be direct. "We heal as quickly as possible, and we go back to fight."

The vampire leaned back in his oversized chair and crossed his legs. "Are you fucking kidding me? We were all nearly burnt to a damned crisp. Now we're supposed to go back and fight against an army of those assholes?"

Surcy tried to hide her surprise. "We don't have another choice. Without the sanctuary, it won't be hard for Caine and his angels to find us. We need to act quickly."

"You mean it won't be hard for them to find us with a spy in our midst."

Her gaze swept to the God of Autumn. "What do you mean?"

The god looked older than the rest, with tangled long auburn hair that fell loosely around his narrow face. His skin was a deep tan, almost the color of the leaves just before they changed shades in the fall. Although he was far shorter than the massive Immortals, he didn't seem to notice or care.

"You might have been able to trick those demons who all have hard-ons for you, but you don't fool us, angel," he sneered. "Caine has been pulling whatever he wants from that mind of yours. That's why the angels found us. That's why we're in danger."

"No—" she denied.

"Yes," he hissed. "And at any point, he can ring his little bell and call you back. And then what? You're his to command."

Was Frink right? The thought sent something aching through her. She'd suspected he was telling the truth... Truth be told, she'd known, but it was too much to consider. If she had to accept that all along she'd been unknowingly hurting her demons... she shivered at the thought. She couldn't. She'd deal with that new emotional blow when the time came.

She drew herself up taller, her heart racing. "I'm here, fighting for what's right. I'm trying to make this world a better place, but I'm not one of you. I can't do this alone. So whether you trust me or not, it doesn't really matter. Do you care about this cause? Do you want to take that bastard down?"

It was the God of Summer who answered. The shifter glanced at her, his golden eyes spinning slowly. "After what he did to me, I would rather die a thousand more deaths than see him remain on my throne. I will kill him, with or without the help of the other Immortals."

"But what about his little security system?" The Goddess of the Ocean stood from her seat, her tail replaced by long legs. "You know that we cannot enter the throne room as long as Caine sits on the throne."

I didn't know that. "None of you can?"

Everyone shook their heads.

Damn it. Then what can we do? How can this work?

And then it hit her, there was only one solution.

Surcy took a deep breath. She knew what she had to do. "But I can."

The God of Autumn huffed. "Yeah, so our plan should depend on an angel Caine can control with a simple word?"

No one spoke for a long minute.

"Perhaps that's exactly what we should do," the Goddess of the Ocean said, her voice holding danger. "Angel, what are you willing to give up for this plan of yours?"

"Anything and everything," she answered with ease.

The woman's ocean blue eyes locked onto hers, and the Immortal crossed the room. Stroking Surcy's cheek, she smiled. "I have a plan, loyal angel. But it will be painful, and it will destroy you."

I've died and had my memory wiped. I've lost the men I love. What more can they do?

Knowing them... something even worse.

Surcy swallowed around the lump in her throat. "All right."

The Goddess turned back to the room. "I know how we can ensure that Surcy is the perfect person to face Caine. The plan is a simple one, but with our help, she will succeed. So, who will join this cause of ours?"

Her words hung in the air.

The Goddess of Love stood from where she'd been seated by the window. Her beauty was so overwhelming it overpowered the room. "All I want is peace and goodness... but none of that will happen until we put that bastard's head on a spike."

The Goddess of Spring laughed. Her solemn expression was gone, replaced by a smile. "I forgot how fucking fun all of you are. I'm in." Flowers sprouted on her fingertips and moved up her arms. "Let's see Caine face us when we're ready for him."

Murmurs rose. Other Immortals stood, moving by the Goddess of Love's side. At last, only the God of the Night remained. And the God of Autumn.

The God of Autumn sighed.

"Autumn?" The Goddess of Love called.

The Immortal glared. "By all logic, we'll lose this battle. And this time when he kills us, it'll be for good. But I for one would rather go down swinging, then hiding like a frightened child. That is your plan, isn't it, vampire?"

The God of the Night rose, his dark eyes locked on all of them. "I'm not afraid."

Surcy stared. "You practically stink of fear."

Anger radiated from him. "I'm going to fight with all of you, but not because of your childish attempts to convince me. I'm going to fight to remind all of you that there's nothing more powerful than the night."

The Goddess of Love moved closer to Surcy, to stand in front of her. "So what's the plan?"

Surcy took a deep breath. *What is the plan?*

20

The next morning, they stood outside the barrier separating Zedussa from the rest of the world. Surcy was positioned in the middle of the line of Immortals. The druids had stayed behind to guard the children, knowing that they might be the last beings with the blood of gods remaining after that day.

Each of the Immortals had donned traditional robes befitting their station. They were long, with slits on the sides, and pants underneath. Each one wore an emblem that symbolized their power. And the fabric was spun of both gold and silver, making it so the morning sunlight seemed to cling to them.

Some of them held weapons.

Some of them were dangerous enough without them.

The Gods and Goddesses of the Seasons would shift into dragons the moment the attack begun. They had no need for anything but their claws and their teeth. It was the same with the Goddess of the Ocean. She no longer wore her mermaid tail, but she swelled with the power of the ocean. She assured them that when the time came, neither Caine nor his angels would be safe from her wrath.

Of all the Immortals, the Goddess of Life was the quietest. She carried with her a golden dagger, but she admitted that she would do little fighting. Her strength would be to lend the others her powers. She would heal their wounds to keep them moving. She was the healer that would fade into the shadows made by the God of the Night.

She was perhaps their most powerful tool.

The vampire stood at Surcy's side with a sword in his hand. He held it like a man unaccustomed to weapons, but he'd reassured her that he could use it, if needed.

The God of Sin, The God of Earth, and The Goddess of Love held their weapons with confidence. Her bow rested in her hand, as if made for her, and she had many arrows upon her back. The God of Sin carried a long sword with a wickedly jagged edge, and the God of Earth carried an axe.

All looked like powerful Immortal beings, ready for an attack.

And yet, Zedussa was silent.

No angels crowded the sky. None even soared overhead. There wasn't even the flicker of movement that said guards walked their paths around the structure.

"It's eerie," the vampire whispered.

She agreed.

"They're waiting for us," the Goddess of Love said, and there was a darkness to her words. "And so we shouldn't disappoint them."

"Just be prepared," The God of Sin said, his voice forcefully casual. "It isn't just Caine and his angels we have to watch out for. His archangel will be there too, and that bastard's smarter than all of them combined."

Surcy shivered, remembering the red winged angel.

When their group started moving forward, she called her soul-blade into her hand. They walked in measured strides across the lifeless lands, moving toward the formidable structure.

"This place was a thing of beauty when we ruled here," The Goddess of Life whispered.

Surcy stiffened, and a strange sensation washed over her. Glancing behind them, she saw that life was blossoming everywhere that the goddess had stepped. Grass sprouted on the ground, hidden seeds split, and trees emerged slowly from their slumber. They grew at an incredible speed, stretching higher and higher as branches and leaves erupted.

Her pulse sped up.

Already things were changing. She prayed that was a good sign.

When they were just outside of an archer's range of the fortress, the Goddess of Love gave an order, "stop."

Immediately, they obeyed.

"It's time," the Goddess of Love said. "We must execute the plan to the letter."

The Gods and Goddesses of the Seasons moved back and within seconds they shifted into their dragon forms. Where once the four Immortals stood, now powerful magical creatures stretched their massive wings. The God of Summer was golden and massive, humming with strength. The God of Autumn was red and simmering with a contained kind of anger, that she could sense waiting to explode. The Goddess of Winter was black, her anger worn about her like a cloak. The Goddess of Spring was a lovely shade of blue, with talons that could sever heads with one swoop.

A cloak of darkness spread over all of them like a black

cloud. For a second, it made Surcy's chest feel tight. The cloud reminded her so much of Caine. But then, she breathed deeply, reminding herself that this was all part of the plan. The God of the Night would do his best to conceal them, for as long as possible.

At last, they were ready.

And then, the war began.

21

Daniel stood like all the other angels. They were silent soldiers, preparing for a war. It took everything within him to stay standing in the silent throne room, knowing that Surcy was somewhere close by, preparing to attack.

This feels wrong. How the hell am I an angel?

A tremor rolled through his body. Images flashed in his mind of the moment he was burned alive.

He felt his eyes widen, and clenched his entire body to keep from throwing up. Was it not enough he had to burn to death in his first life? He'd had do it again!

His head spun, and he felt light on his feet. Burning to death had to be one of the worst ways to go. Even after that, he had experienced a different kind of pain when his soul appeared in the throne room. Daniel had been still withering in agony when Caine had turned him into an angel and wiped his memory.

He'd fought it with all his might, but it was useless.

He would never forget the moment he tried to kill Surcy.

It would haunt like a ghost for the remainder of his life. He didn't know how she'd brought him back, but making love to her was the only thing that healed his soul. That kept him from imploding the moment he realized all that had happened.

Thank God for Surcy.

Staying by her side was the only thing that could bring him peace again, yet he was more valuable here. He had to pretend that he didn't remember and be ready to help her when the time came.

Even if it drives me mad.

Even though not knowing what happened to Mark and Tristan was its own kind of torture.

Suddenly, Daniel sensed a change in the room. His gaze moved to the darkness that concealed the cowardly Caine, and his entire half of the throne room.

What's happening now?

Caine's darkness crept slowly out over the rest of the room like a cursed mist. It did nothing to hide the red-winged archangel that leaned back arrogantly near the bastard, nor did it hide the three portals to the other realms.

Despite himself, Daniel's gaze flickered to the portals. They loomed deadly, salvation and punishment, the blinding brightness of the entrance into the angel realm, and the absolute darkness that led to the demon realm. Beyond them was the Soul Destroyer, closest to the back of the throne room. It hummed of danger.

"They will be here soon," Caine said, his voice breaking the tension-filled silence. "There's more that still must be done."

The doors to the throne room opened, and four angels carried a massive wooden stock across the room, before setting it near the portals. They opened the top, where spots had been made for a head and hands to go.

He's going to punish someone? But who?

"Daniel."

When Caine said his name, he knew. He knew that the punishment was meant for him. And yet, how could Caine know that Daniel's memories had returned? Daniel had done everything that was asked of him. So was this about something else?

It doesn't matter. I have to obey.

He stepped forward and bowed, even though it was like a dagger in his stomach.

"Yes, Caine."

"Go in the stock." Caine's command seemed to fill the air.

He didn't force Daniel to obey. The demon could try to fly or outrun the six dozen angels who crowd the room, but Caine and Daniel both knew he wouldn't make it more than a few feet before he was dead.

So, Daniel played his game. "Yes, Judge."

He went to the stocks, placed his hands and his neck into the carved out spots, and held himself stiffly as it was closed over him and locked.

"Good. Now, the bait is ready. We need only to set the trap."

Fuck. Is he going to use me against Surcy?

His stomach clenched, and he made a silent prayer. When the time came, he hoped Surcy had the strength to let him die again.

She had to.

If he distracted her for one moment, he knew Caine would win.

Clenching his fists, he shifted, testing the strength of the stocks. They held, without the slightest leeway.

His mind began to spin. There had to be a way he could still help Surcy. *But how?*

22

Surcy watched as the dragons unleashed their flames on the fortress. The God of the Summer latched onto the roof of the structure and began to pull, his massive wings flapping, causing wind to press down on all of them. The other dragons seemed to understand. Their flames stopped, and they latched on too.

The entire building shuddered and shook. Angels came pouring out of the hole in the center of the roof. They attacked with their flaming swords, but fire blazed over them, killing them instantly.

Surcy held her arm over her face, wincing up at the chaos, and then, the roof came tearing off. One of the Immortals shouted. They ran, throwing themselves on the ground. Stone fell like rain from above them, and she held herself tensely, hoping nothing hit her.

Several quiet moments passed before she looked up. The entire roof of the structure was gone, most of it tossed to the ground on the other side of the fortress. Stone had fallen all around them, but to her complete shock, none of the Immortals seemed injured.

They rose once more and moved to the massive door of the structure. She tensed wondering how the Immortals would open it, when the doors were flung open, and angels came pouring out.

The God of the Earth swung his mighty axe. Heads fell.

The God of Sin was there to defend him, to watch his back each time he swung his axe. And the Goddess of Love shot her arrows, each one hitting an angel with ease.

She clenched the handle of her sword more tightly and took a step forward as the God of Night's darkness spread around them once more. When the first angel swung at her, she avoided his blow with ease. They danced around each other, jabbing out, swinging their blades, connecting over and over again.

And then, water struck him in the back. The angel hit the ground, and Surcy severed his head in one blow.

Turning, she spotted the Goddess of the Ocean. Water swelled behind her. Gathering water from a nearby source, she held it back like an invisible wall. She shot out little streams at the angels who attacked.

All around, the Immortals fought like animals, distracting the angels.

Surcy took a deep breath. *It's time.* This was the part of the plan that terrified her the most. None of the Immortals could enter the fortress until Caine was removed from the throne. While they could battle the angels and cause a distraction, she would have to take down the Judge himself.

I just hope this plan will work.

Teleporting, she appeared just outside the throne room doors. She had no idea what she would face inside, but she knew the task was hers alone. Then, slipping the little bottle from her pocket, she stared briefly at the dark liquid swirling inside.

Tears stung the corners of her eyes. She removed the cork, took a deep breath and chugged it down.

Gagging, she forced herself not to hurl the disgusting liquid. She only had one shot at this. And it had to work. Instantly, her lips began to tingle, and her gut began to churn. Time was of the essence. Already she could feel the chill moving through her body, spreading out to find its source. Tossing the bottle on the ground, she knew it was time.

Pushing open the doors, she tried to enter as quietly as possible, but the noise of the room immediately exploded around her. Her jaw dropped. Above the huge room, angels fought in the air against the dragons who blasted fire, and chomped them in their massive jaws. It was bright, and warm from the dragons' fire.

Not at all like the throne room that haunted her nightmares.

Her gaze moved to where she would find Caine. To the man she must take down.

Time stood still. Daniel was encased in stocks. At his sides? Mark and Tristan stood with their flaming swords pointed at their friend. The dark liquid in her stomach churned faster, and she felt the chill moving up her spine.

It was impossible. All three of her demons had been turned into dark-winged angels. None of their souls had been destroyed. Mark and Tristan hadn't been given the special water, so they were both mindless soldiers. It was clear that Caine intended for them to be Daniel's executioner.

The cruel bastard.

"Welcome, Surcy," Caine said, his voice uncurling from the darkness. "The time has finally come, the moment that will finally end this rebellion once and for all."

She swallowed hard. *I can't look at my demons. I can't worry about them. They're simply distractions.*

"It's time for you to step down and give the rightful judges back their thrones."

He laughed low, as if angels and dragons weren't fighting above him. "None of the Immortals can face me, and so, this plan of theirs hinges on *you* taking me down. Do you really believe you have any chance at succeeding?"

"No," she said.

Her confession hung in the air between them.

His dark cloud moved towards her, and she sensed him drawing nearer, stopping just behind her angels. "I can't imagine they sent you here unprepared."

Was there fear in his voice?

"They did not."

"Come here," he ordered.

Gritting her teeth, she fought his command, but it flowed over her, through her, racing in her very blood. She struggled against each and every step, yet she struggled in vain. Within moments, she was standing before the dark cloud. Close enough to touch her demons. She felt Daniel's gaze upon her. It took everything inside her not to look in his direction.

"Kneel before me," Caine said. "And let me pluck their plan from your thoughts."

His words weren't a command. She glared at him. "Not a chance in hell."

"Such an attitude," the voice came from the darkness, and her eyes flicked to the red-winged archangel.

Every instinct within her screamed. She hadn't expected to find him here. The Immortals had thought he'd be leading the battle, but they should have known better.

"Coward," she hissed at them. "Hiding in here when there's a war to fight."

The archangel smiled, his expression slimy. "I live only to serve the great Caine." His tone was filled with mockery.

"I told you to kneel," Caine said, but she could almost feel him smiling as he said it.

"No fucking way!" she shouted at him, itching to call her soul-blade into her hand, to sever the heads of these two monsters.

"Why not just command her to?" The archangel said, but she got the sense their words were rehearsed. That they were playing with her.

"You know what might be more fun?" Caine asked. "We should let her make the choice—this foolish cause of hers, or the loves of her life."

Her heart pounded. The dark liquid's chill was everywhere, bleeding from her blood to something deeper, perhaps her very soul. Her teeth began to chatter and her limbs began to shake.

"Just face me like a man!" She shouted. "I'm tired of your games and bullshit."

"Mark," Caine ordered. "Hurt the angel."

Despite her every intention, she turned. Mark had the same subtly handsome face, the same gentleness to his features. Although his glasses were different, the way they framed his deep blue eyes was as familiar to her as her own.

He showed no emotions as he drew the sword deeply across Daniel's hand, drawing dark red blood.

Daniel jerked in the stocks. His jaw clenched and pain shone in his eyes, but he said nothing.

"Stop this," Surcy said, and she didn't have to fake the emotion in her voice.

"Only you can stop this." The humor in Caine's voice made her want to tear out his throat.

"Mark, Tristan, you were once demons, fighting for our cause. Daniel is your best friend. You can't do this. You can't hurt him."

Tristan raised a brow, his stoic face expressionless. She looked into his mismatched eyes, craving to see recognition in his gaze more than she needed air, but there was nothing. A wicked déjà vu flowed through her but she pushed the feelings aside. She would deal with them later.

"Kill him," Caine ordered.

Her soul-blade leapt into her hand, and she caught Tristan's blade with her own one second before it touched the back of Daniel's neck. Tristan pressed down harder. She fought against his strength, even as the blade lowered, cutting a line of blood into the back of Daniel's neck.

"No," she sobbed.

Inch by inch, Tristan forced her blade deeper.

Daniel cried out.

Surcy did the only thing she could think of to end Daniel's suffering. She sent her soul-blade away.

The power of Tristan's strength sent his sword down in one quick, fatal motion. Daniel was dead. His body still hung there, lifeless, held up by the stocks around his wrists.

She couldn't look at his severed body. A sob exploded from her lips as she turned away.

"One down, two to go," the archangel said, laughing.

Overhead, a dragon's roar echoed with rage. Whether it was for her loss or his pain in the battle, she didn't know. She kept her focus on the archangel.

"Why are you doing this? Fight me!"

"Oh, but that's what you want, isn't it?" Caine said.

She stiffened, but tried to hide her thoughts. Did he

know what they had planned? Did he know that the Immortals had discovered a simple way to destroy him?

"I could order your demons to walk straight into the Soul Destroyer. I just have to wish the portal to open and it is so. They can't refuse a direct command. Then they will be gone."

"No," she denied him, her stomach turning. "You can't."

"Go to the Soul Destroyer," Caine ordered Mark and Tristan.

They obeyed him without hesitation, coming to stand close to it. Instantly, the portal seemed to open. Darkness moved from it like a black fire, licking at their legs and feet. Their dark wings shook upon their backs, but they remained in place.

"Let me see their plan, or I will forever destroy the two men you hold so dear."

Tears filled her eyes. With the slightest order, Mark and Tristan could be lost to her forever. She couldn't make a mistake now. Too much was riding on her getting this right.

As tears ran down her cheeks, she collapsed onto her knees. "Do it, if it will keep Mark and Tristan safe."

The darkness pulled back from Caine and she saw the face from her nightmares. His haunting beauty whispered of death and danger. He placed his big hands on either side of her head and tore into her mind like a savage.

Surcy screamed, the violating feeling making revolution blossom within her. For one long minute, he peeled through her chilly thoughts. He froze.

His confusion was like a perfume that filled the room. He slowed in his exploration of her thoughts, focusing on the moment the Goddess of Life filled the bottle with its dark liquid. The substance had only been used twice before in the history of forever.

"No," he whispered.

And then, he was shooting out of her mind.

"No!" he shouted, staring at his hands as the dark veins appeared, spreading onto his fingers, wrists, and up his arms.

Spinning to his archangel, he shouted. "You're the only one powerful enough to take this poison from me. So take it!"

The archangel smirked and stepped away from him. With a simple gesture, Mark and Tristan flew across the room, slamming into the stone.

"What are you doing?" Caine shouted, true panic in his voice. "If I die, you go with me. They'll execute you as a traitor."

His smirk widened. "Or I can do what I always wanted… serve no one but me."

The archangel leapt into the Soul Destroyer. For a minute he screamed in terrible agony as it ripped at him, and then, he was gone.

Caine turned to her. The black veins had spread up his neck and gathered on his face. The black veins spidered in the white of his eyes, and then his head tilted back.

A second later, he collapsed to the ground.

So did Surcy. The poison the Goddess of Life had used to infect Caine through Surcy was a powerful one. It wouldn't just destroy him. It would destroy her too.

They'd warned her they didn't know what would be left of her to be reborn.

Her breath puffed out in front of her and tears flowed from her eyes, tears of relief and sorrow. It was done. Caine was destroyed. The Immortals would take control again, and everything would be different.

Better.

So much had been lost.

But all that mattered now was that it was done.

Closing her eyes, she knew the instant the poison consumed her entirely, because there was nothing. Nothing left of her.

Then came the darkness.

23

Mark screamed as the Immortal touched his head. His memories exploded in his mind, and then, it all came back to him. Surcy. Daniel. Tristan.

Everything.

Including the fact that Tristan had killed Daniel.

The Immortal drew back his hand. The being's golden-eyed gaze held his. "We, the Immortal Ten, have been restored to power. You are an angel who will serve us."

Mark nodded, even while he tried to force air into his lungs. He'd killed Daniel. He'd worked for Caine. He'd betrayed everything he'd ever believed in.

And yet... his memories were fuzzy. The Immortals had won. Caine was gone.

He should be happy.

Turning, he saw that Tristan was kneeling beside him, recognition in his eyes. So his gargoyle brother remembered it all too.

Now what were they to do?

"You may rise," the Immortal said.

They both stood.

"Go and find a place," he commanded.

They turned to see lines of white and dark-winged angels lined up perfectly in the throne room. They found a place in one of the lines and waited, for what they didn't know.

From behind them, a line of people walked on a path through the angels. When they reached the dais, they spun. All wore matching golden robes. Instantly, he recognized the Immortals they had saved. The ten most powerful beings in existence sat upon ten golden thrones that had been concealed by darkness for far too long.

The God of Summer remained standing, staring out at the ranks of angels. "We are the Immortal Ten. We have ruled here since the beginning of time... until the usurper Caine came. He was the child of the God of Sin and the Goddess of Winter, a being with the unexpected ability to manipulate minds. He used his powers against all of us. He manipulated our thoughts. Some of us he killed over and over again, ensuring we remained ignorant of who and what we were. Some of us he manipulated into prisons of his own making, but he made a fatal mistake. He knew that the Goddess of Life had had a child... but he did not understand her role in restoring us to power."

The God of Summer gestured with his hand and suddenly a woman appeared, surrounded by dark-winged angels. She blinked in confusion.

"Where am I?"

The Goddess of Life stepped forward and smiled. "Daughter, Goddess of Hope, you are home."

But there's already ten of them. How can there be more?

"I don't understand," she said.

"The Goddess of Life concealed your father. Caine

believed you to be an Immortal, but he didn't understand that you were more powerful than the ten of us... because your father wasn't a simple mortal." He hesitated. "It's me."

The woman's eyes widened, and Mark recognized her as Sharen, the demon-hunter that Surcy had saved many times before. She was an Immortal?

An *eleventh* Immortal?

"Come to me, daughter," the God of Summer said.

Sharen stepped forward, but three massive angels stopped to block her path.

"What do you want with her?" One of them asked, the defiance in his voice surprising everyone in the room.

The Immortal smiled. "Not to worry, Alec, she is safe."

Alec didn't move. A small hand grasped his arm and pulled him back, and then she walked forward, lit by the same inner glow as the other Immortals.

Without being told, she knelt.

Her father smiled. "There are only ten thrones. Ten judges to decide the fate of man. To make you a judge would destroy the balance." His gaze moved to the Goddess of Life. "We have decided how to ensure you may survive within this world, but not overthrow the balance. You, my daughter, will help with the great changes that will now occur. Many demons will be angels soon, and many angels will be demons. Someone with knowledge of all the realms will need to help with their adjustments, while we focus on our job—to judge mankind."

She looked up at him. "I can do that. But not alone."

"Then, you will have your lovers at your side. Not ours to command, but yours."

A surprising smirk touched her lips. "I'd prefer they be given free will."

He raised a brow. "Are you certain?"

"Yes," she said, with absolute certainty.

"Is that all?" he asked, and there was a fatherly humor in his voice.

"I'd like Surcy and her lovers too. This is a big job, and I could use an angel I trust at my side."

His smile faltered. "You may have her lovers, but not Surcy."

"Why?" she asked.

"Because Surcy... she has been reborn as an angel. But she paid the ultimate sacrifice in this war. Her mind is gone. Who she was. Not just her memories. Everything."

Sharen rose, her jaw clenched. "Bring her to me."

Her father raised a brow. "My daughter, we have all tried to restore her mind."

"And yet none of you are the Goddess of Hope." Tears gathered in her eyes. "She gave up everything, father. Everything. I may have set this rebellion in motion, but she restored all of you to power. Surely I can try?"

He nodded and made the slightest gesture.

Two angels hurried from the throne room.

Mark looked from one Immortal to another. He realized he'd been in shock. Nothing Sharen had said had made sense, but now he realized, and the knowledge was like a hand plunging into his heart. Surcy... she didn't remember them. *Again*?

How could it be possible? Were the Fates simply cruel children playing their heartless games?

The doors opened once more and one of the angels came in carrying Surcy in his arms.

Tristan sprung forward and snatched her from the other angel. His eyes were wide, fixed onto her face.

The other angel returned a moment later, leading

Daniel. Daniel looked confused. How long ago had the Immortals brought him back?

Daniel and Mark hugged, a hard hug that said what their words couldn't.

They all three stood together, looking down at Surcy's face. It wasn't like before, when she had been confused and didn't recognize them. . It was... blank.

She stared off, as if seeing nothing.

"Surcy," Tristan whispered, the word torn and filled with tears. "Surcy!"

"She can't hear you," The God of Summer said. "She can't hear anything anymore. She is just a shell. The essence of Surcy—whatever made her at her core—is gone."

"Bring her to me," Sharen, The Goddess of Hope, ordered.

They moved up to the dais with even steps. If Sharen couldn't fix her, no one could. That knowledge made him feel as if the world was crashing down on him.

Tristan laid Surcy at Sharen's feet and the goddess knelt down, touching her gently.

Mark spoke before she could act. "If you can't restore her mind, I want your word that you'll destroy mine."

"And mine," Tristan and Daniel repeated without hesitation.

Sharen's eyes filled with unshed tears. "You can't mean that."

"Promise us," Tristan said. "Give us the word of an Immortal."

Sharen looked up at her father. After a moment, he nodded, but his expression was reluctant.

She took a deep breath, and reached out to touch Surcy's head. Her eyes closed, and minutes of silence ticked by. Her expression changed, from faraway to frustrated.

Come on. You can do this. Save her life. Bring her back to us.

At last, Sharen's eyes opened. "Something's wrong."

Her father spoke. "I told you. It isn't possible."

"It's not that," she said, and then her gaze met theirs. "I can't bring back someone I didn't know that well. But you all can. Touch my hand."

They obeyed without question, placing their hands upon hers. One second they were in the throne room, the next they were gone, pulled through their lives with Surcy.

He remembered when they saw her on that farm, many years before, the most beautiful angel in existence. One who let them live for reasons none of them would ever understand.

Their memories ran through every laugh, every tear, every small moment that meant more than the big ones, every piece of themselves that contained Surcy.

Someone drew in a deep, shaky breath, but they kept being pulled through time, pulled through everything, until they reached the end. Until they reached that very moment when they touched Surcy, their hearts in their hands, ready to die for her.

Mark opened his eyes. Surcy was breathing hard, her eyes closed. Her entire body shaking.

His gaze met Tristan's and Daniel's. *Did it work?*

Sharen suddenly collapsed. Her demons—no, her angels—surrounded her, pulling the little woman into their arms. Sharen wasn't looking at them. Her eyes were on Surcy.

"Come on," she said. "Come back."

"Surcy?" Mark said, taking her hand. "We love you. Are you in there somewhere?"

Very slowly, her eyes opened, and they were staring at two pools of the deepest blue. "Mark?"

It was like an explosion in the room. Tears filled his vision, and he pulled her into his lap. They gathered around her, kissing every inch of her. Glorying in the look of recognition on her face.

And then, she laughed.

"What?" Daniel asked.

"You all make the strangest looking angels."

And then, they were all laughing.

She touched each of their faces. "And I remember. Not just this, but before, before Caine took my memories."

What must this be like for her?

It was something they'd have to deal with, not now, but soon. But they would be there for her, and they would be there for each other.

The God of Summer came to stand closer to them. "My daughter truly is the Goddess of Hope, and she's given it back to you. Now I must know, can you serve my daughter as she helps to fix these shattered realms? Can you follow her of your own freewill?"

"Freewill?" Surcy asked, confused.

"You won't have to obey anyone, angel."

Surcy nodded. "I can do that."

"And so can we," Mark said, without hesitation.

The Immortal smiled. And then, a flash of light came over them.

This time, it wasn't the end. Just the beginning of something more.

24

S urcy smiled as she stared from her bedroom window. Plants, trees, and flowers spread out in all directions, growing from the ash. It would not be the druid's sanctuary for Immortals anymore. Instead, it was the place they would train angels and demons who had been placed in the wrong realms by Caine.

They weren't able to help every demon and angel. Some of them couldn't be pulled from the realms, for reasons the Immortals had not yet determined. They believed it had something to do with the Fates, but none of them were sure.

And yet, they were able to help most of the people and to begin setting things right. It was everything Surcy had dreamed of and more.

Because she wasn't just an angel bent to the will of new masters. She was working with Sharen, by her own choice.

With her demons... well, her *angels*, she corrected herself with a grin..

And life, it was actually pretty damn good.

The door of her room opened. Mark, Daniel, and Tristan came in, their dark wings folded upon their backs. Her own wings shivered. She was still getting used to having them back, a gift from the Immortals themselves. There was something strange about not only having them, but seeing her demons with them too.

Daniel grinned. "Sitting in here staring at your wings again?"

She laughed. "I am not!"

"Then, you're waiting for us," Daniel's smile widened and he looked to the bed.

Despite herself, a tremor moved through her body.

"Oh, that's exactly what she was waiting for," Tristan said, his voice deepened by arousal.

Too proud to admit it, she turned casually and sat on the edge of their big bed. "I was just going to take a nap."

"A nap?" Mark asked, too innocently.

She began to undress, removing her clothes in moments. "A naked nap."

"A *naked* nap?" Daniel sounded horrified. "Without us?"

She stretched and crawled into the bed, tucking herself under the covers. "I'm pretty tired. Long morning and all."

"Fuck this," Daniel said, and then he was tearing off his clothes.

Surcy had to hold back a laugh as he came sliding into the bed.

She wanted to tease him, to torture him, but the second his lips found hers, all thoughts of waiting died. His kiss was so hot, deep and desperate, and everything she loved about him. When his tongue swept inside, she was lost, lost to his touch.

She was lost until she felt his big hand sliding down the valley of her breasts, down her belly, and then to the junction between her thighs. When he began to stroke her slowly, she gasped against his mouth. Her thoughts spun, and she arched against his touch.

The big bed shifted as Tristan knelt, naked, at the edge. She moaned again with her eyes closed, and Daniel kissed her again. She felt Tristan lift the blanket, and thought nothing of it until his mouth pressed inside her wet folds.

One man stroked her, one man sucked her, and the sensation was incredible. Life-altering.

She moved against them, growing closer to her orgasm with each second.

When Tristan plunged his big fingers into her body, she broke their kiss and began to swear. Mark sat naked on her other side, he caught her lips and his kiss was different... gentler, slower, like an intricate dance. His hands found her breasts, and her nerves screamed as he brushed her nipples with his thumbs.

"Fuck this," Daniel groaned.

And then, he moved her. Tristan lifted his head from between her legs, and everyone moved back as Daniel came behind her. Immediately she knew what he was doing. She gripped his thighs as he lowered her ass onto his hard shaft.

She was tight, struggling to stretch around him. Then Tristan's head was back between her legs and the tension eased. The discomfort passed as they gave her everything she needed.

When Daniel reached his hilt, they were both breathing hard. He laid back, gripping her thighs and spreading her wider. Tristan gave her one last hard lick, and then, he moved higher. When he positioned his tip at her entrance, she felt overwhelmed. Could she handle feeling this good?

He plunged in hard and fast, and she cried out, her nails cutting into his shoulders. And then the two men were inside her, moving as one, awakening a higher level of pleasure that she chased like a drug.

"Mark," she moaned.

He moved closer, and she dropped one hand from Tristan's shoulder and began to stroke him in slow, even strokes. Her druid groaned, and then they were all working in a rhythm, nerves firing, bodies slapping together. Sweat ran down her back, and Daniel parted her ass wider from behind, his thrusts into her harder with each second.

She felt a ripple over her skin, felt her orgasm building.

"Mark," she moaned again.

He rose up on the bed and plunged his cock into her mouth. She took him deep into her mouth, the salty, sweet taste of him an addiction. Her arousal grew as she felt him hard and swelling. When he grabbed her hair into his fist and began to thrust harder and she melted at the sensation of him dominating her mouth.

She loved having all three cocks inside her.

Her orgasm came like a wave of pleasure, an explosion of her body reaching the ultimate level of pleasure. The men followed, filling her with hot cum... the evidence of their own pleasure.

She held them close, shaking and crying out around the cock in her mouth as she came. It lasted too long, wonderfully long, until she came back into her body and felt them around her.

Mark laid at her side. They stroked her flesh, and she snuggled between them.

It felt like she was... home. It felt... right in every way.

Which was exactly the instant someone knocked at her door. "Surcy," a deep voice called. "You're needed outside."

"While you do that, we're going to take a little nap," Daniel muttered.

She pulled out from between them and whirled on him. "*I* was going to take a nap."

"Well, there's no sleep for the head angel," Daniel said, smirking.

She punched him playfully in the shoulder. "You're going to pay for that."

His handsome lips curled into a smile. "I'm looking forward to it."

25

A white-winged angel with hands bound knelt outside their new home. Ranks of angels stood behind her, and one angel stood at her side, using his magic to keep her from teleporting.

When she looked closer, Surcy recognized the bound angel. She was the blonde who had helped distract Frink when she saved the kids.

"We caught this traitor," the angel at her side said, his voice filled with anger. "The Immortals will wish her instantly thrown into the demon realm."

Sharen met Surcy's gaze, and she slid closer.

"This is the same woman who helped me when I rescued my demons," Sharen whispered in a soft tone.

"She helped me save the Immortal's kids."

Sharen sighed. "She was also the bitch who told them I was heading to save my demons in the first place."

"So what do we do?"

Sharen didn't speak for a long time. "The second she's turned over to my father, her life will become hell. I'm not sure she deserves that, but she doesn't deserve to remain an angel."

"That doesn't answer my question," Surcy said, with a humorless laugh.

"Take her to the dungeons. Untie her hands. Tell her that soon she'll have a chance to escape, and to take it. If by the time she's caught again, if she hasn't found a way to redeem herself, then we'll have no choice but to condemn her to the demon realm."

Fair enough.

Going to the angel, Surcy grabbed her arm and started toward the little dungeons they'd had built.

"So what's my future?" The woman asked, tension in her voice.

"That's entirely up to you." Surcy cut the ropes from her wrists and shoved her into the prison. The angels there kept a ward up that prevented anyone from teleporting out. "When you have the chance, better get going, and find a way to make up from the wrongs of your past."

The prison doors shut on her confused face.

Surcy turned and started back toward their home. Angels practiced in the field, some of them from the demon realm, some of them new. But it didn't really matter.

All that mattered is that a new era had been born where the right people had been placed in each realm. Innocents were no longer being tortured, and cruel people were no longer in positions of power.

Now, when the angels fought to keep humans safe from demons, they were doing what was right. The balance had been restored. Even though there would be more battles in the future, the war had been won.

Yes, the thought of the archangel in the realm of the Soul Destroyer sometimes kept her up at night, and she worried that there were still powerful angels and demons who had remained in the wrong realm. For now, this was enough.

Entering the massive house, she moved through the halls and up the stairs. When she opened her door, her three angels were in a mass of snoring, naked flesh. She smiled.

This was her own kind of heaven. The perfect one.

IF YOU ENJOYED THIS BOOK, **check out more books by Lacey Carter Andersen.**

If you en

ALSO BY LACEY CARTER ANDERSEN

Secret Monsters

Unchained Magic

Dark Powers

An Angel and Her Demons

Supernatural Lies

Immortal Truths

Lover's Wrath

Legends Unleashed

Don't Say My Name

Don't Cross My Path

Don't Touch My Men

The Firehouse Feline

Feline the Heat

Feline the Flames

Feline the Burn

Feline the Pressure

God Fire Reform School

Magic for Dummies

Myths for Half-Wits

Mayhem for Suckers

Alternative Futures

Nightmare Hunter *audiobook*

Deadly Dreams *audiobook*

Mortal Flames

Twisted Prophecies

Box Set: Alien Mischief

The Icelius Reverse Harem

Her Alien Abductors

Her Alien Barbarians

Her Alien Mates

Collection: Her Alien Romance

Steamy Tales of Warriors and Rebels

Gladiators

The Dragon Shifters' Last Hope

Claimed by Her Harem

Treasured by Her Harem

Collection: Magic in her Harem

Harem of the Shifter Queen

Sultry Fire

Sinful Ice

Saucy Mist

Collection: Power in her Kiss

Standalones

Worthy (A Villainously Romantic Retelling)

Beauty with a Bite

Shifters and Alphas

Collections

Monsters, Gods, Witches, Oh My!

Wings, Horns, and Shifters

ABOUT THE AUTHOR

Lacey Carter Andersen loves reading, writing, and drinking excessive amounts of coffee. She spends her days taking care of her husband, three kids, and three cats. But at night, everything changes! Her imagination runs wild with strong-willed characters, unique worlds, and exciting plots that she enthusiastically puts into stories.

Lacey has dozens of tales: science fiction romances, paranormal romances, short romances, reverse harem romances, and more. So, please feel free to dive into any of her worlds; she loves to have the company!

And you're welcome to reach out to her; she really enjoys hearing from her readers.

You can find her at:

Email: laceycarterandersen@gmail.com

Mailing List:

https://www.subscribepage.com/laceycarterandersen

Website: https://laceycarterandersen.net/

Facebook Page:

https://www.facebook.com/authorlaceycarterandersen

Printed in Great Britain
by Amazon

86256231R00089